Winter
Tales

Kenneth Steven lives on an island off the west coast of Scotland. He is a poet, children's author, novelist and translator: some thirty of his books have been published to date. He travels widely to undertake readings and give lectures and creative writing workshops, and he has made many programmes for BBC Radio. Much of his writing is available on Kindle. <www.kennethsteven.co.uk>

Winter Tales

KENNETH STEVEN

Marylebone House

First published in Great Britain in 2017

Marylebone House
36 Causton Street
London SW1P 4ST
www.marylebonehousebooks.co.uk

British Library Cataloguing-in-Publication Data
A catalogue record for this book is available from the British Library

ISBN 978–1–910674–50–5
eBook ISBN 978–1–910674–51–2

Typeset by Manila Typesetting Company
Manufacture managed by Jellyfish
First printed in Great Britain by CPI
Subsequently digitally printed in Great Britain

eBook by Graphicraft Limited, Hong Kong

Produced on paper from sustainable forests

This book is for my mother,
to thank her for the inspiration of stories
through all the years of my childhood

Contents

Preface

For a long time I feared that short stories would remain always beyond my pen. I loved them: I read the work of Katherine Mansfield and all the Russian greats; I discovered the stories of American authors like Hemingway and Scott Fitzgerald. I fell in love with stories like 'Ethan Frome'. But still I didn't seem to be able to create my own.

The short story has been described as a little novel. It is a window; a tiny moment that is sufficient to open the senses and the heart of the reader to what might become a whole world. It is no more than a look into a secret garden, but sufficient to convey the scent and wonder of it before the door is closed once more.

I think that what finally helped me write my own stories was the translating of them from Norwegian. Some years ago I had the honour of bringing the Nordic Prize-winning novel *The Half Brother* to English. But the author, Lars Saabye Christensen, is in my opinion first and foremost a writer of exquisite short stories. It was these I wanted to translate more than anything – and I did, without ever finding a publisher willing to bring out a collection.

Preface

The paradox is that the translator often works with the text of a short story or novel more intensely than the author. I lived with those stories for days as I worked on them, sentence by sentence. I have always felt that this process helped me understand the short story in a way I simply had not done before.

But there are still days I despair and fear another story will not happen again. I am only thankful for the ones that have poured from the pen, and those contained in this selection represent the ones that have truly won their spurs.

A good number have been read on BBC Radio 4; several have been published at home and others abroad. 'The Ice' was nominated for a Pushcart, having appeared in an American journal; 'The Listener' was runner-up for the V. S. Pritchett Memorial Prize.

Often the stories seemed to appear from nowhere and write themselves on the page in my tiny cabin in Highland Perthshire, where nothing disturbed them until they were done. My thanks to all those who read those first drafts, and offered wise advice on their completion.

Cullen Skink

I t was a day in November such as only the north-east corner of Scotland can endure. The wind came in what he called tufts, chasing smoke from roof stacks and sending gulls at angles into driving mist. The sea was a living cauldron; from where he stood above the town he could see no boat pitching and diving through the waves. And what man would want to be out there, yet generation after generation of his family had sent their sons to pull a living from the deep. How many lay at the bottom of that endless heaving of water they called the Widowmaker? Had he not been a fisherman himself for nigh-on twenty years?

Peter Jonah Mackie turned back up the road. He didn't want to think about the sea; too much of his life was lost to it already. As he raised his head to keep walking the steep road, his eyes met the steeples of no less than six churches. They were a God-fearing folk in the town of Cowie, and up and down the coast it was little different. When your lives hung by a thread, there was nothing for it but to pray the boats would make it back through the storms another year.

*

1

Jonah had been his grandfather's middle name before him. As a boy he'd carried the name with pride. When the minister spoke of Jonah and the three days and nights he'd spent in the belly of the whale, his cheeks had burned. He'd imagined Jonah lighting a fire inside the whale, and the great fish in agony beaching on a rocky islet so Jonah could walk ashore.

He'd always imagined that on the headland called Spurn Point. A place of criss-crossing tides, made of nothing but granite stacks and boulders. You could see no dwelling from deep down in the hollow of Spurn Point; Cowie was swallowed by the cliffs. It felt as old as time, and it was here he'd wandered alone as a child. East of here nothing but what his grandfather called the grey wolf of the North Sea, and beyond – Norway.

How could it have been that twenty-four and a half years later he'd return here, just after dawn, to find the body of his only son washed in after three days missing at sea? The *Mary Jane* lost in the worst winter storm, and his son's wife at home in Cowie, six months pregnant with their first child. How do you begin again after that? What do you say that fails to sound wooden and hollow and barren?

'I'm home, Calum,' he said softly, closing the front door, and the boy who was his grandson came charging into his arms so lemons and onions and salt went rolling over the floor from his bag. How do you begin again and what do you say?

*

The boy's mother had had to get a job at once; there was no time to grieve. She studied at night in the room that had been her husband's workshop. While Calum Iain Mackie slept, knowing nothing of the world he had come to, having chosen not a shred of the story that was his. It was a strange net that had brought him up to the grey streets of Cowie.

His mother was out teaching now; Peter had two hours with his grandson. They played well together; he got down on his hands and knees to be lions and tigers – raced along the corridor on all fours until Calum rolled about laughing. Peter laughed too, though there was something like glass inside; he laughed as he tickled the boy yet still it hurt. But by the time Ailsa had returned from school they'd be sitting on the sofa together, Peter reading and Calum perched beside him.

Today wind and weather chased about Cowie; a day for being cosy and forgetting. For a time at least, before the real world and its sadness came blowing back through the front door.

'You're going to sit up here and help me, Calum.' He hoisted the boy onto the work surface beside the stove, then remembered his grandson wasn't ready.

*

'This is for you,' Peter told him, putting on the play apron with blue and white checks Ailsa had found for him in Aberdeen. At that moment, all that interested Calum were the contents of a jar of raspberry jam; he was concentrating on digging out the last little bit and lifting it to a sticky mouth. But Peter took the jar from the starfish hands and the blue eyes watched him now, little feet jigging over the side of the work surface.

'We are going to make the best soup in the world, Calum Iain Mackie! And you are going to help me!'

The small head nodded contentedly as a gull blew past them over the next garden, and the telegraph wires whirled like skipping ropes.

'We'll need a lot of tatties! And your mother dug these from the garden only yesterday.'

He held up a bucket of potatoes for Calum's inspection – peeled and ready. Carefully they rumbled into a pan of bubbling water. Calum searched for a last piece of jam at the end of one finger.

'Now, this is the bit you're going to help me with. Watch carefully. I'm going to start with the smoked haddock.'

He waved strips of fish under the boy's button nose that wrinkled as the scent rose. Calum did nothing but watch as the strips were cut into tiny yellow cubes.

'Wait until you smell this, my wee fighter!' Peter exclaimed, eyes sparkling. He poked Calum's tummy.

'We need plenty of the best butter, and we melt it till there's nothing but runny gold in the pan. What I want is the pan to be hot, but not so hot the fish burns. That would be bad, bad as you losing a marble under the sofa you never found again! So you just put in the bits of fish – gentle, gentle. See how they're yellow to begin with? They must be white by the time they're done, and break into pieces with the wooden spoon.'

'When will it be ready?' Calum asked, and looked up from under his white-gold curls. His dad had been just as fair when he was five years old. But his hair was the colour of winter beech leaves by the time he left school. By the time he'd told them he wasn't going to Aberdeen to study; he was going to fish out of Cowie and was saving to buy a boat called the *Mary Jane*. Peter swam back into the kitchen and the moment; heard the echo of his grandson's words.

'It will take exactly long enough,' he answered. 'The best cooks can't tell you how long things take to make, Calum,' he went on as the tiny fragments of fish squeaked and squealed in the pan. Gently he moved them to one side and then the other with the wooden spatula.

'They take as long as they need. Sometimes they need longer and sometimes they're finished before you know it.'

*

A bit like life, he wanted to say. *A bit like this strange journey we're on called life, where everything you plan can change in the blink of an eye, and the only real certainty is what happens at the end. And I wish I could preserve you from all of it, but I can't. I wish I could take your hand and tell you there was an easier way, because I love you with all my heart and I want to keep you from the rocks. If there's anything I want, it's to keep you from the rocks.*

'Now,' he said instead, 'what we need next is a tiny bit of onion. Not enough to ruin the taste of the fish, because that would be awful! Just this much, Calum – enough and no more. Will you come down and help me, because you can't where you are! You're up somewhere about Ben Nevis, and that's no good when you're helping make the best soup in the world. Wait till I find you the stool.'

Carefully he lifted the boy so his little feet stood sure and safe on the wooden stool that had belonged to his mother, and maybe to hers. It was scuffed and scarred so it was worthless, yet he'd fight the man who tried to take it from him. It was priceless, and somehow inside was all the labour of the mothers that had gone before. He kept it in honour of them.

'Hold the wooden handle tight as you can, and stir the onion and the fish together. That's it! I'll put my hand over yours and we'll do the rest together. Don't stop! A bit more and it'll all be melted and ready! Well done!'

He ruffled the corn-coloured curls and Calum looked up at him, gleaming.

'But you're not done! Oh no, the most important thing is still to come. This is from the recipe for Cullen Skink that goes back to the time before Mary Queen of Scots was thought of.'

Peter held out in front of Calum a whole lemon and let it roll over his palm.

'This is the secret,' he whispered, 'and you're going to make the magic come true. Stay there and let Granddad do the difficult thing first. This is the dangerous knife, and you never do anything with that.'

In a second he'd cleaved the lemon in two.

'Right, time for the magic! Squeeze with all your might and the secret lemon will trickle through all that fish!'

Calum ginned. His half of lemon was dented, but it needed a strong hand, and Peter's came round his own so juice dribbled and ran. He said nothing as he concentrated and watched, and he thought of his son's hands as they must have fought that night on the *Mary Jane*, and he felt the sting in his eyes. For a second he couldn't see his own hand over Calum's; they became one and flowed together, until he heard the boy's delighted joy as the last of the juice ran out. Then they did the second one and by that time the storm in Peter had stilled and his heart had slowed. He could be himself, as though everything was all right and nothing was wrong inside. The way he had to be for this boy now, until he was old enough to understand.

'No one else knows the secret,' he said, bringing the boy down from the stool. 'And it's as old as the salt in the sea!'

Calum's eyes were dancing now. 'What do we have to do next?'

'There's one amazingly important thing left,' Peter told him. 'No, that's not true – there are two. But first we put the fish and the onion and the magic lemon in with the tatties, and you can stir it all like a witch would stir her magic broth!'

Calum stirred as if life depended on it, held up in his grandfather's quivering arms. Peter brought the boy back to the floor with gratitude. Ailsa wouldn't have let him do that, he was sure. She guarded her boy like gold. But what could you say? Could you tell her she was doing Calum no favours? You had to watch and be patient. You had to remember and do nothing but love.

'And the very last thing we do, my wee fighter! We take a whole carton of cream and slowly pour it in. We take the pot away from the heat to let it cool, and we put the lid on tight. Yes, you can do that – I'll lift you up and you can make sure it's tight. Oh, what is that mother of yours feeding you? I'll soon not be able to lift you at all!'

*

Then they were done and the whole house smelled of lemon and fish and cream. Outside rain hurled itself against the glass, and the sea went wild. They sat together and read a story; Calum's index finger following the words. Ailsa would soon be home and the three of them would have Cullen Skink. He cut big chunks of fresh bread and put a plate of them on the kitchen table. Suddenly he thought of something, a question he would dare to ask.

'And what are you going to be when you grow up, Calum?' He bent down close to the boy; felt the sharpness at the back of his eyes, his heart hammering his chest. He bit the edge of his lower lip.

Calum's eyes rippled with gold, and for a second – no more – a pale, damaged edge of sunlight broke from over the sea.

'I'm going to be a cooker!' Calum shouted, dancing in his apron, and they laughed and they laughed and they laughed.

Elmeness

It was always twenty past six when Annie woke. It was the robin outside her window, in the rowan tree. She knew he came to waken her and sometimes, when she opened one half of the curtain, she would see him there on one of the branches, before he flew away.

It was Saturday this morning and there was nothing she needed to do. She didn't have to find kindling for Aunt Isobel's fire, nor did she have to do homework because there was no homework to do. She felt that feeling of Saturday morning at twenty past six flow into her tummy like a kind of honey. She sat at the window for a moment, her elbows on the sill, and looked out over the whole of Elmeness. It wasn't high summer any more; the year had started to crinkle. That was how her grandfather described it and she could hear how he said the words as he tapped out his pipe by the stove.

The robin had gone from the rowan tree and she saw how the berries had turned orange; only a week or so ago they had been yellow. And she was sure there was something different about the sky, as if the light and the clouds had changed, though she didn't quite know how. At that moment, the sun bloomed full through Elmeness and Annie thought how silly it was to be sitting there when she could be outside instead. And she was dressed sooner than it takes to riddle a chimney. That was something else her grandfather said, but even he didn't seem terribly sure what it meant.

She put on everything except her shoes. Aunt Isobel was almost certainly awake and reading some favourite book or other, but Annie wanted to think she might be asleep just the same. There was one particular stair she knew she had to avoid; if you stood on a certain part of it there was a noise like a tummy rumbling. She carried her shoes all the way downstairs, and once when she wanted to sneeze because of the dust, she pressed the forefinger of her right hand (the hand that was empty) under her nose so that the sneeze would go away. That was a trick her grandfather had taught her one day when she was feeling very sad; he said it was useful if you were borrowing biscuits from the tin at the time.

*

Outside was a thatch of birdsong. She clicked the door shut as if she did not want to disturb the world. It was like when the first snow came; she always walked along the stones at the edge of the drive, because the pure whiteness was too perfect to break. One day, when she had become an artist at eighteen, she would paint the scene so it was captured for ever. She would paint Elmeness so everyone would know how special it was, for Annie knew that it was really the centre of the world and always would be.

But now it was just the first day of autumn. She slipped on her shoes and began running, right under the great beeches. They made a great shingling in the breeze as if to welcome her, as though they had missed her and were welcoming her back. Under their huge boughs were flickerings of sunlight; the whole ground was freckled with shadow and sunlight. She would paint that too, she thought, and she imagined capturing the colour of those flashes of sunlight – gold with an edge of red.

She looked up and there he was, as though she had known he was there. Acorn the red squirrel, balancing on a branch as he swayed backwards and forwards in the breeze. Aunt Isobel had laughed and said he would make a good sailor; he would have run up any rigging there was. And Annie laughed now; she clapped her hands and Acorn was off along one branch and leaping away to another. Sometimes he sat and chattered to her, and she liked to imagine he was bringing squirrel gossip, all the stories his paws could carry from the local village.

But today he was away like a flame, up into the rigging of the beeches, and had no stories for her at all. She had drawn him once for her art teacher in school, in the ten minutes at the end of the lesson when they had nothing else to do but could practise on scraps of paper with their charcoal. Old Grump had gone to the headmaster with it later the same morning. He had knocked and gone in and put it down on the desk in front of him, and let the sketch by Annie Gilmore speak for itself.

*

And the headmaster, who didn't like being interrupted by anyone, child or teacher, looked up at him with open blue eyes. There was no doubting where Annie was destined, if she kept her hand to the plough and didn't look back. For they knew what a weight of sadness she carried; the smallest child who had been given the biggest burden. But they couldn't bring her parents back; they could only give her the tools to carry into the world that lay ahead of her. Old Grump never actually said anything to her about the drawing, of course, though he may have been a little gentler when she came forward to ask for more paper that last Friday before the holiday began.

Then the wind was still and Acorn was gone. She turned round as if she knew for sure, and there was Aunt Isobel's face at the window, smiling, and Annie began running, because she knew there would be white rolls for breakfast and that the fire would be lit. Most of all, more than anything, she knew it was still the holidays for another nine and a half days, and that felt like the sweetness of butter on her tongue.

The Skylarks and the Horses

I t was only a day after he arrived that they were brought to the hospital. It was late October and children were getting ready for Halloween; their piles of branches and leaves had melted into pathetic lumps in the woods. There was flooding all round the hospital; at least one road was impassable. In fact that's why they arrived so late that night; it was navigating the back roads that took so long.

John Aitken was still up reading case notes. He wanted to finish the notes of the last two patients before going to bed, but he also wanted to know when the men arrived. But by half past ten his eyes were blurring, and at twenty to eleven he got up and opened the window. It was an old trick he had learned when an undergraduate at Queen's, working on essays that had to be delivered the following morning: an open window and coffee.

He opened the window now despite the rain that was still coming down in stair rods, and it was at that moment he heard the car whining up the hill. The porch was suddenly flooded with light and there was Savage down below, all five foot two of him and the moustache bristling.

The car stopped and a couple of nurses bustled out into the half-dark beyond the porch. There was the muffled sound of voices; theirs and those of the men or the driver. John Aitken kept standing at the open window; they had returned from the trenches to this.

Savage was already making his speech, about the fine traditions of the hospital and how some of the best in the land had worked here on troubled minds for more years than he cared to think of. The four of them were in a line, beyond the porch and still in the full force of the rain. He could see one of them, on the left-hand edge and closest to him, all bent over. He must have been a foot and more taller than Savage and suddenly he began weeping; he started this uncontrollable weeping and it threatened to drown out the words of the doctor. Without warning, Savage turned and struck him full across the face. After that everything was confusion; Savage's speech ended, nurses bustling about and everyone talking over each other. The half-light of the porch was a blur of shadows.

John Aitken closed the window and kept standing there. The fountain pen lay below him across the page, useless and empty. The last two sets of case notes lay unread. He went to bed and lay in the darkness, asking questions to which he had no answers.

*

One of them wasn't able to get out of bed, not without help. He lay there as though constantly freezing cold, shivering uncontrollably. He always lay in a certain position on his back, facing just slightly to the right; his head raised as though he was trying to get up. That was how he was the whole time he was awake.

Beside him was a man who seemed almost not to be there at all, as though everything that had been inside him was gone. It was only a shell that was left. He reacted to nothing, not even Savage's commands, and no one knew what had happened to him. Yet the irony was that he looked whole; the skin of his face shone and there was an absolute serenity in his eyes.

The third man spoke, but not when he was spoken to. He talked into thin air, about his brother who had a garden and kept chickens, who had a bicycle that was missing the bell. He talked about Brenda who had always liked him and who was waiting for him to come home, who would be there on Friday when he got off the bus and gave her the flowers. And he talked about his brother who had a garden and kept chickens. He never listened to what anyone else said to him and he fell asleep as though someone had cut the strings that supported him, slumped right over and was gone.

Beyond the wards was a long corridor, roofed with glass and with glass windows. Beyond that lay the garden. There were four wicker seats there. It was in the fourth of these, the one furthest away from the entrance to the corridor, that Ruary preferred to sit, looking out into the garden. He seemed somehow even bigger there; that great head and the blue eyes, watching the garden.

As though something was there or would be coming soon. But he was calm, as long as no one was in front of him blocking his view. Otherwise he would search past them, not interested in what they offered or wanted. He had to see into the garden.

*

'Dr Savage?' Aitken, the new doctor, stood in the doorway.

He came in, whether he was welcome or not; clicked the door shut. Savage motioned towards a chair and moved a mountain of paper on the desk.

'I've been working with nervous conditions over the last year, mainly with men sent home from the Front. Some of the changes have been remarkable. We're still learning but it's been exciting.'

'So you've been sending them back in their droves to fight?'

A slight pink to the cheeks; a shifting of the feet.

'No, that's not what I meant and it's never been my intention. My hope is to get them well. Above and beyond that . . .'

'So what do you see here, Dr Aitken?'

'Well, I wanted to say that I've found it best to work with one patient intensively at a time. To devote complete attention to that individual. Find out as much as I possibly can . . .'

Savage leaned over the desk towards him.

'I haven't had the luxury of that kind of time! Perhaps you in your city hospital were able to work like that, but this is a different world.'

He paused, sat back in his chair again. He had been there once upon a time, in the seat Aitken was in now – literally and proverbially speaking. It was easy to forget.

'Ideally you may be correct. But this war is hardly giving us time like that, when cattle-loads of shattered men are being sent home day on day. You can't even talk about weeks now. It's every day: every single day.'

They agreed on that, but there were no two ways about it.

A silence; the sound of Joan's voice half-muffled in one of the corridors. That was Joan's voice. He shifted in his old chair.

'There's one patient I'd like to work with in particular, Dr Savage. Ruary MacLennan. I'm not about to let that concentration of attention have any kind of impact on everything else I'm doing . . .'

'Well, I don't think there's a blind thing you'll be able to do for him, but I can't stop you. As long, as you say, that it doesn't affect the rest of things . . .'

Aitken got up, nodding – a brightness in his face. 'Thank you, sir – I appreciate that.'

'And, Aitken, one other thing.'

'Yes?' He had his hand on the half-open door.

'Nothing. It doesn't matter.' The eyes were grey.

*

It was a week later the snow came in earnest. All across the Highlands so the roads closed. They filled in one by one and it was as though the world went back to what it once had been. Everything was far away again. The power went, snuffed out by fallen telegraph poles and broken branches. He sat at his window one Sunday morning, blowing warm breath onto the patterning of ice on the inside of the glass, until he could see the world. That silence which comes with snow, which is even bigger than silence itself. And he thought of his nephew on the Western Front, and how the snow would be falling there, across the pointlessness of another winter of war. But it was as if the skies beyond his telescope's view had no news; they were utterly still and there was no news.

A gentle tap at his door and words he couldn't hear. He shook himself from his reverie and got up, called that he was coming.

'Joan.' He had learned her name because she was pretty. Well, he knew everyone's name now but hers had been the first.

'I'm sorry to disturb you, Dr Aitken.'

Should she not have been at church? He thought he and Savage were the only ones who absented themselves from the church pews on a Sunday. Perhaps it was the only thing that united them.

'You asked us to tell you if there was anything we knew about Ruary.'

He nodded, letting her speak. He would have asked her in, but that would have been folly. It was brave of her to come to his door.

'I didn't know if you knew that his first language would have been Gaelic.'

He nodded, not because he had known, but because he agreed. It mattered, it made a difference. Ruary MacLennan was from South Uist, an island whose population was almost entirely Catholic – well nigh a piece of Ireland that had floated off the map. Of course he would have grown up bilingual, yet sometimes after a crisis a person would revert to their mother tongue. Was that where Ruary hid now?

She was silent, still looking at him from the shadow of the corridor.

'Well, thank you for coming to tell me, Joan,' and he smiled, beginning to shut the door.

'There's something else.'

She looked at him as though that was all she could say, as though she had brought him something he would have to translate. Her eyes . . . her eyes full in the shadow of the corridor.

'Come in, Joan!'

He made toast and tea, stirred the fire to bring from it an orange glow. He said small things to settle her, gave her a plate, let her spread the butter. The tea so hot it burned the mouth. And then she looked at him again and he leaned closer. She had to begin; he could not do this for her.

'It's my brother, Dr Aitken. The brother who was here – Iain.'

He nodded. He remembered him. He had come with a food parcel for Joan from the Isle of Skye. And he wasn't long back from the Front. He'd been quiet; hardly said a word.

'He saw Ruary.'

'How d'you mean, Joan – I don't follow. Tell me.'

He had asked them to tell him anything. It was like finding keys to a door that was locked in many places. To find a way in.

'He saw Ruary out there. He remembered him. When he walked through the corridor he passed him, and he knew he had seen him before. Then someone came out and said his name.'

'What did he say, Joan? Tell me everything he told you.'

'My brother was coming back; he couldn't remember the name of the place. A ridge. They'd been there all day just getting ready for some big attack. They were coming back – Iain said it must have been about six o'clock and they were so hungry. They were trying to take a short cut through this bit – I'm sorry I'm telling it so badly, Dr Aitken – I wish Iain were here to tell you himself.'

He wished that too but he shook his head. 'You're doing fine, Joan. None of this I would have known. All of it matters!'

'Well, they passed this point where Iain says they were pulling a man back from no-man's-land. It was raining, really pelting rain, and they were dragging him backwards, dragging him by the heels – and they were saying his name the whole time. That was how Iain remembered, because he'd never heard that name in his life. And the man was just weeping and weeping.'

She looked into the golden core of the fire, her hands curled together in her lap. He nodded, thinking and searching.

'And what was he doing? Why was he out there?'

'Iain said there was a horse. He couldn't see properly because it was getting dark, but he could hear this horse. It was crying. It was out there crying and he had gone out to try to rescue it.'

'How did he know all that, Joan? How could Iain know if they were just passing through?'

'I'm not sure, Dr Aitken. I wish he were here to tell you.'

He shook his head. There was no point pushing. He had to help. It *was* a kind of translation. She had brought it to him.

'All right. So perhaps the way was blocked and they couldn't get through. They had to wait and that was when they brought Ruary out, because he must have seen him properly if he recognized him the other day.'

'Yes,' she said, looking up. 'They were talking all around him, the men who were bringing him out. Talking and laughing. Saying that was all he cared about. The skylarks and the horses. That he wasn't interested in anything else. That he just wanted to rescue everything he could.'

She was pleased. He could see that she was pleased it had come back, that she had found it. They had found it.

'Thank you, Joan,' he said softly. 'Thank you for the courage you had to tell me.'

*

That night he had a particularly vivid dream. He was on a hillside and he knew that he was desperately thirsty. He blundered into a ditch and began walking its length, until suddenly he realized it was the bed of a dried-up stream. He hadn't noticed it before; he had blundered on, thinking about nothing but his burning thirst, kicking stones and anything in his path to one side. He stopped and looked down at the trench, the trench that was actually the bed of a dried-up stream. He bent forwards and saw that a whole world lay before him.

There were tiny fern-like plants that had curled in on themselves; there was the pattern of where the water had run through a silt of tiny stones and fragments of silver that were mica. He found himself bending right down until he was actually kneeling in the stream, looking in wonder at all of it.

He woke up and lay thinking a long time, until he was aware of a chinking sound around him. This old part of the hospital was never silent: the pipes, the floorboards and the doors – all of them seemed possessed by spirits. But there was something else and at first he couldn't decide what it was. A chinking that became a kind of song as he listened.

And then he realized what it must be. He was hearing drops of water from all the corners of the roofs outside. The snow was melting at last. And then he remembered that he was thirsty.

*

The room had a glass window, a single square pane of darkened glass – a kind of spy-hole. It was a place from which to watch; a kind of eyrie. The air was bad in there, almost thick, he thought. And when you looked out of the window it was like peering out through some kind of early diving helmet. It felt underwater in there, and the world beyond had a darkness about it, a thick darkness, and all sounds were muffled. You couldn't hear voices properly.

And suddenly he thought of what his nephew had told him of the gas attack; the fumbling for helmets and the under-sea world they swam in. The strange sounds of voices beyond; the swimming forwards through yellow fog.

He sat up, brought himself back. He watched the man outside, the tall young man who sat in the fourth chair in the corridor, looking out into the garden. As though he was waiting, waiting and watching.

You wouldn't have thought there was anything wrong with him as he sat there serenely this mild morning. The blue eyes in the wide face; the big hands on each arm of the wicker chair. He was all right; as long as his vision was not blocked, or anyone tried to move him. Savage had done it; two days ago they had been on their rounds and Savage had wanted to get him up so he could be taken for a bath. He began pulling him, pulling him up from the chair and talking all the time – insistently, fiercely. Ruary had curled away from him, putting up his hands to protect himself and to go on looking ahead, whimpering all the time.

Savage lost his patience and slapped him. 'Get up, man! I've asked you three times and I'm not asking you again!'

Ruary curled away from him, one arm trying to shield his face. He slid deeper into the chair, as though that way he could escape, as though that way he could become smaller.

'What seems to be the matter?' John Aitken had been in the ward and came out; couldn't ignore it any longer.

'Nothing is the matter, Dr Aitken.' Savage didn't turn round.

The younger man paused, then bent down and put his hand on Ruary's right arm. He talked to him quietly; what words they were didn't matter.

'You are interfering, Dr Aitken, and I told you not to.'

He came back to himself in the small room, the diving bell. He knew a little and he needed more. Was it ever possible to know everything, to know everything truly about the working of one single mind? And even when you knew everything, did it mean you would find the answer?

The man with the corn-bright hair sat still in the chair that was his, looking out for ever into what he saw somewhere ahead of him.

*

A letter came from a Mr Norman MacLennan of South Uist, saying that he would be coming to Inverness on Friday 14 December. Would Dr Aitken be so kind as to meet him at the Station Hotel? It was written beautifully, the half-page of words, but the address in the top right-hand corner had been smudged and was illegible.

Savage assured John that if he were to write a card to Mr Norman MacLennan, South Uist, it would reach him without a shadow of doubt. So he did, lacking the faith to believe it had the slightest chance of falling into the right man's hands.

But it was good to leave the hospital that Friday all the same. There was plenty of snow still in the higher hills, but sunlight came in sweeps over the Moray Firth and there was a strange mildness to the air that made it feel more like the other side of Christmas. How had Norman MacLennan of South Uist known where Ruary was, far less the name of his doctor?

Perhaps it was this bizarre Highland world at work again; a small parish where news seemed to spread before it had been properly thought out, and where you couldn't speak ill of anyone because the chances were you would be distantly related to them.

The Station Hotel was clouds of white rolls and kippers that morning. There was soft laughter at tables; the murmur of half-heard talk. His eyes circled the corners for someone who might be Norman MacLennan, but the man was already struggling to his feet. There was something in his face that was the same, but he was smaller than Ruary and wider; he had spilled over his edges. Cheeks and hands ruddy and puffed. They sat down and coffee was brought; he allowed himself a white cloud of roll.

'They say he's gone queer. Is that true?'

He had to wait until he had swallowed, but it let him think. It was most certainly the war that had done its damage; that was for sure. Something very serious had happened that had affected Ruary. That was why he was being cared for where he was.

Neither a nod nor an answer; just the look of the two blue eyes.

'Are you related to Ruary, Mr MacLennan?'

'I'm his uncle, brother to his father Sorley.'

'Then why don't you come to the hospital to see him for yourself? It's only half an hour out of Inverness . . .'

'No, I had only this morning and I need to be back on the island by tomorrow, Dr Aitken, so this was a chance to hear how he is.'

He had seen it all before and the signs were classic, textbook. That was fear speaking; the fear of being infected by whatever it was that had affected his nephew. No need to come too close.

He had done his duty and could say so; he had abided by the letter of the law. At the table behind they were leaving, apologizing as they began moving great chestnut-coloured trunks. It gave Norman MacLennan the chance to say something else, to escape into laughter.

'May I ask you if Ruary was popular in school?'

The eyes blinked. As though the question didn't make any sense.

'Ruary was different. He was brought up on a croft that was right beside the seas. He was out on the water from the age of four and learning about boats. He's happier on water than ever he'll be on land.'

'So he'll be a good swimmer?'

The face was aghast and the eyes searched. 'Certainly not. That would be the last thing he would learn.'

They were like different creatures. He was from the land and this man was of the sea. As though they didn't quite understand each other, were just out of earshot. Like two men shouting from different cliffs, never catching all of the words, building their answers on what they thought they might have heard.

He had to try to find a way in, to unlock something. 'What about his family, his parents?'

'They loved him very dearly.'

Again the defensiveness, the misunderstanding. He was about to say something and he didn't, because MacLennan hadn't finished.

'He was very close to his parents. He learned everything he knew about boats from his father, and he lost him when he was fourteen. They were out on the water together and Ruary came home alone. It would have been around that time he tamed an otter. It went with him everywhere – on the boat, in the house. The otter would only listen to him. He had a way with animals, a great fondness for them. But there's no use telling you that.'

He was embarrassed, as if he had said too much. It was as though you could see him closing, folding in on himself having become self-conscious. As though he had betrayed something.

'And his mother, Mr MacLennan. Is she still alive?'

'Yes, yes, of course. She's on her own in the croft house.'

But all at once he had become aware of the time and it was useless, pointless.

Suddenly John Aitken was on his own outside and a fine sleet was falling in the sunlight. Sunlight was being blown through the town and there was new blue sky up above. He buttoned his coat and began back to the car, still hearing the sea.

*

He saw her shadow in the garden as he was putting out the last lights at midnight. He had spent an hour in the little room with its thick window of dark glass, and he had asked himself if that was how he saw the world. He spent an hour there doing nothing but sitting, looking out into the corridor and the fourth of the chairs as it stood there empty.

But now he saw her shadow in the garden. Crouched there on the edge of the path, at right angles to him now as he stood in the middle of the corridor and its glass roof. For a second his eyes didn't see her as real; she might have been a carved figure there in the darkness, frozen completely as she crouched, staring straight ahead.

'Joan?'

She turned round and was real, got up and started over to him.

He realized he had hardly spoken to her since that Sunday morning when she had had the courage to come to talk to him. He didn't truly know her, and yet he felt he did.

'Why were you out now? What on earth?'

'Feeding foxes.'

But the smile was crying. He touched her arm, searching, and they went inside. He shut out the mauve shadows of the trees, the mildness of the night.

'What is it? Tell me.'

Their voices soft and low in the corridor beyond the wards. Perhaps it helped they couldn't see each other properly there; they were shadows, their faces were dark shadows.

'Dr Savage,' she said, and bowed her head, bringing one hand over her face. 'Dr Savage's son Michael.'

'I didn't even know he *had* a son! What about him?'

'You didn't know because nobody knew. Well, they knew he had a son, but he was never talked about, never mentioned. He was at boarding school in England and when he came home he shouted at his father, told him he hated him. He went out as an officer the day the war began and his parents never heard anything; he refused to write. Dr Savage wrote to him every week.'

'How do you know all this, Joan?'

He knew that her face was looking at his; he saw the grey shadows of her eyes and they seemed much bigger in the darkness.

He wanted to say something more and he couldn't; he only stood, waiting for her to speak at last.

'I'd prefer not to say, Dr Aitken.'

Said in one breath and he nodded, even though she could not see such a thing. He nodded and it was all right.

*

It was the night of the flood. The night that the Deveron burst its banks, the night the Spey overwhelmed Aviemore. It was the night that left the River Ness in spate, and a young boy out taking nothing more than oatmeal to his grandmother was swept away and never found. His parents weren't even able to grieve over a body.

He was aware of the rain at first without understanding it. The song of it there, hour after hour, in the stillness of the night. He could not sleep. He was curled away into himself, hearing the soft thud of his own heart.

Then he really heard the rain, the hammering of it on the roof and its singing from the crow-stepped gables and in the gutters. And for a second he seemed to hear a crying and he sat up, bolt upright, and everything made sense at last. He dressed, quickly and silently, went out into the hallway and put on his shoes, his hands trembling as he tied the laces. He pattered down the steps and made his feet softer on the gravel as he walked, as he went towards the porch and the main hospital doors where the men had arrived all those weeks ago on just such a night as this.

He went inside and knew he would find Ruary there; he had seen it the moment the rain had made sense. That tall figure in the wicker chair crying as though his heart would break, staring out into the invisible night of the garden as though back on another night, in another place. Except naked now, completely naked as he sat there watching and waiting for something that would not happen.

John Aitken crouched in front of him so he did not block his view, and he took his hand in his own.

'Come on,' he said softly, 'I'm taking you home.'

Lemon Ice Cream

I f I close my eyes now, very tightly, I can smell everything. The ice cream that my father is scooping into bowls in green-white curves, the little kitchen with its open dishes of herbs and its baskets of vegetables. The windows are open and all of us – my mother, my brother, my father and me – we are all looking out onto the umber sea of the fields, and the scent that is coming in is from the lemon grove.

I used to get up early in the summer to walk there, just to be there. To lie on my back and listen to the shingling of the leaves and let that scent, the scent of the lemons, fill me completely. And at night when I couldn't sleep in my tiny room under the attic, I would open the latch of the windows and let in the lemon breath of the dark.

I was four years old. Born in Sicily under the shadows of the mountains. My father called Mount Etna the blue ghost. And when I was five we left, all of it was taken away as suddenly and completely as a teacher wiping a blackboard. There were little finches my father fed; they came to one of the windows at the very top of the farmhouse and he fed them. Most of the other boys had grown to love hunting such birds; netting them and caging them. But my father had a soft heart; he could not bear to see such beautiful things hurt, and he fed the finches. It was the last thing we did before we left, him and me; we stood there with our palmfuls of seeds, me stretching on tiptoe, the tears on my face. His voice was so soft; those words of kindness he whispered both to the finches and to me. They were for both the finches and me.

We were leaving for America, for New York. It was a time of new hope, new dreams, and no dreams came bigger than America. And the last thing my father took from that farmhouse, that place that had been home to six generations of our family, was the recipe for lemon ice cream. I don't know where it had been hidden all that time; it was as though like a magician he snapped his fingers and brought it out from behind his ear. Yet there it was, in an old square envelope, with flowing writing on the front. And his dark brown eyes shone as he showed me.

We sailed to America. Everything we could carry was stowed beneath us in this great ship ploughing towards the New World. Marco and I ran everywhere – he was nine and I was five. This was our ark; we had set out across the sea for a new world and everything we needed was on board. We went down as deep into the ship as we could, to beside the great engines that roared and shook like angry dinosaurs. We went up to the highest deck and watched the grey swaying of the sea, and the brown smoke fluttering from the funnel.

*

And we smelled New York before we saw it. We smelled it and we heard it, Marco and I. Very early one morning when the sea had become a pale piece of glass, we scurried up from our cabin, went on deck and leaned out, and we smelled and we heard New York. It was such a mixture of scents, such a tumbling of things, as though an old bin full of rubbish had rolled down the side of a hill. You tried to catch things at random and always it went on rolling. The bin never stopped tumbling out of control, for ever. Hot smells and sour smells and burnt smells and fresh smells and dead smells and new smells. They made us excited, they set us on fire, but my father hushed us as he leaned out too, for he was listening to New York – he was hearing the city.

'Those are the biggest sounds in the world,' he whispered to us, and somehow we believed that they must be, that they were. He quietened us with those words, he made us listen, and the smells and the sounds gave us pictures in our heads – pictures in ochre and bright green and orange. But when we came to New York a fine rain was falling, a mist like a mesh of flies that seemed to dampen the scents and the sounds and leave only the great looming greyness of the skyscrapers.

We came to our new home, four flights above the street. On the other side of the hall were the Pedinskis, and above us there was nothing but the roof space and the sky. The only place we had to play was the stairs, and we made it our train station, the launch-pad for our rockets, our cave system, our battlefield. On four flights of stairs were Jewish children, Polish children,

Italian children and German children. We had nothing but our imaginations and the days were not long enough. We ate each other's food and we never went hungry.

One Saturday in the hot summer we had been outside, all of us children. We came back panting, full of stories, and sat on different stairs, leaning against the wall. My father came out with bowls of lemon ice cream, his ice cream, and as soon as I bent my head to that bowl I smelled home. I was back in the kitchen, I was up feeding the finches, and I was down in the lemon grove. The tears flowed from my eyes and he comforted me. He rocked me in his arms that evening until I fell asleep.

He kept the recipe behind the old carriage clock in the living room. That brown, crinkled envelope. Sometimes if there was a high wind in the autumn, the fall, and the draught crept under the front door and through the top of the high windows, I would hear it rattling behind the clock, dry like an ancient seed pod. It was there behind the clock, the clock that never lost a second's time, that flickered its passing segments of time like hurrying feet. The clock and the paper.

*

Then, one spring, my mother fell ill. Everything was beginning again, coming alive, after the long winter, and it was as though she went the wrong way and couldn't come back. It was as if we kept moving and had to watch her getting further and further away, disappearing into the snow. I remember her waving to me as I set off for school in the morning. The pale oval of her face behind the glass, trying so hard to smile. That is how I saw her; that was the last memory of her every day, that painting of the pain of her smile. I remember going with Marco and my father to pray for her in a little chapel at the heart of the city. I tried so hard to pray but my head was full of the evening traffic, the shouting and laughter outside. I wanted so desperately to guard her and keep her safe from harm in that place, but not even there was there sanctuary.

My father seemed to grow old in front of us after she died. I remember thinking that one night when we sat together in the living room: *the clock and my father are set at different speeds*. One night I had a dream, a particularly vivid dream. It was of a field, a great wide field. I could see nothing beyond it; it was the only thing there was.

And I came on my father in that field and he was planted in the ground. Mad as that sounds now, he was planted in the ground. And I began digging out his hands and feet, his wrinkled fingers and toes, and all the time I was thinking to myself: *this soil is wrong*.

I was twelve years old. Marco had left school and couldn't find a job. My father, who had worked on scaffolding high above the city, who had sat and laughed with friends on beams the width of a leg half a mile over the streets, he had grown afraid. He had lost the courage to put one foot in front of the other.

Lemon Ice Cream

That winter the snow fell and fell and fell. The skies were quieter than silence itself and the flakes spun like ballerinas from the sky and buried the world in white. The noise of the city diminished bit by bit; like a great, old animal New York lurched into its own cave and went to sleep.

The wind fluttered the curtains in the living room. It was six o'clock in the morning and I stood there alone, twelve years old and hungry. My father and Marco were asleep. There was nothing left in the house to eat. The wind came again and I shivered; there was a rattling and it was the old envelope behind the clock, the recipe for lemon ice cream. I felt sadder than ever before in my whole life; it was as though there was only one colour in the world now, the colour grey. And I made up my mind. I felt behind the clock and I found the piece of paper. I put on my shoes and I went out into the grey, sleeping morning with that crumpled paper held tight in my left hand.

*

And I sold it; I say no more than that I sold it. I do not even want to think of the people to whom I went, nor the place where that was. All of it still hurts too much; it is like some red sore where new skin will never grow again. It is enough to say that I was paid a bundle of dirty notes. I caught the smell of them as I took them and I felt sick. It was the smell of the subway, the smell of the basement where no light ever reached. All the way home my hands smelled of it too, and I wanted to wash them clean; I wanted to scour them until it was no more.

Even as I came inside I felt sick, but not only with that terrible smell. I felt sick with something else and I sat by the window; I hunched there and cried and cried and cried.

Outside, the new day was just beginning; there were voices and sounds and scents. The first light came red and beautiful through the streets, beams that crept and changed all the time.

And when I stopped crying at last I looked down on all of this and I thought: *the snow and the light are bigger, they are bigger than all of us together.* For there were men toiling in the snow, digging out cars and pushing them and swearing at one another and at their wives. Taxi drivers in their yellow cabs were shaking their fists and yelling. They were blinded by the red light that came low through the city; they tried to shield their eyes and they had to stop. All they could do was shout and swear, and I looked down on them from where I was four flights above, and they seemed so small and what they struggled against so huge.

I looked up and listened; I listened to the one room and I listened to myself. I felt utterly empty. I had cried myself dry; my eyes were empty caves. The dirty banknotes lay strewn over my lap and some were scattered over the floor at my feet. They were like leaves that had blown in the window – old, dead leaves.

My father and brother would be up soon; my father to sit in the living room and look at pictures and wait, just wait; and my brother to drag on his coat and go out into a city that did not want him.

Except that everything had changed now. I looked up and I listened and I realized I could hear nothing at all. The clock had stopped ticking.

The Song of a Robin

I remember the day I left. I was seventeen and I hadn't told them. I remember the look on my mother's face; she was cutting bread and turned round – a white oval of surprise. She cut herself and was crying, and I thought to myself: *is she crying because of what I've told her or because she cut herself?*

My father was stacking wood with my brother in the yard, and they looked round at me too. I don't remember now if it was because I said something or because my mother called to them. I remember it as a kind of dream as I left the house; when I think of it I am swimming through the kind of sound-lessness there is in dreams. And their faces, my father's and my brother's, are still following me as I walk away. They have blocks of wood in their hands and they are turning all the time to follow my leaving.

It is 1914. Why am I going? Why do I leave a sleepy village at the edge of a sleepy county to join something that means nothing to me whatsoever? Is it because I am tired of going out to fetch water at dawn on white mornings when there is nothing but the cold rawness of the wind and the stink of chickens on the breath of it? Is it because I want to believe in the talk around huddled beer tables, the lure of somewhere else and somewhere new? Perhaps I am no different from the seventeen-year-old boy in Athens who heard the stories of warships and swords, and whose heart raced at the sound of the words. Or is that only an excuse?

I am cold and I wish they would bring me a blanket! Where is anyone in this damned place? They should be here by five-thirty and it's ten past six! There's a robin there. Out on the window ledge. Wanting crumbs no doubt. Go and beg from someone else! You won't get any from me.

There was one we fed that first winter, poor fools that we were. The following winter there was next to nothing for ourselves; we would have had precious little compassion for a bird. But that winter he used to flutter down at five past eight each morning, right into our trench. I can see the faces watching now, faces of men who were to die in the long months that followed. Their faces are a strange photograph inside the book of the memory, as they watch a robin eat crumbs from the palm of a man's outstretched hand.

*

A man who is ready to take up a gun with a bayonet and rush across no-man's-land to kill and maim all that stands against him. And the men he is preparing to gouge and rip and blow apart have done him no more harm than that simple robin. He has no reason to hate these men, and the chances are that he will never make it far enough to see their faces.

For this is what war is about, otherwise it would not work. After that first football match on Christmas Day in 1914, the officers had to pull rank; they had to order their men back into the trenches to begin again the task they had come to complete. In case peace had broken out like spring flowers all the way along the Western Front.

I realized all too soon my folly in running from home to this. Often enough I felt like the prodigal son, and yet had I gone on my hands and knees all the way to my father's house, there was nothing he could have done to save me from my fate. I had grown up on a farm and I had known small horrors: I had seen pigs whirling about long after their throats were slit, I had seen animals caught in traps – traps I had set myself. But now there was horror all about me; there was no release from it by day or night. For the few hours one managed to sleep, dreams were horrified by the cries of men who still lay undead in no-man's-land, hopelessly lost in a sea of mud and barbed wire and other men's blown-apart bodies.

And dream I did. Perhaps in the end we dreamed the same dream, up and down the line and on both sides of the trenches. I had been crazy about a girl called Anna in the village since I was twelve or thirteen. She had wild gold hair and eyes the colour of soft blue, eyes that always were dancing. And I dreamed one night that she came to find me, to bring me home. I was the only one awake in my dream; everyone else lay asleep all along the line, and a kind of frost covered their faces and their hands. I heard Anna's singing far away (for she was forever singing) and perhaps it was that magic that put everything else to sleep. Because goodness and beauty could not live in this place, it was impossible.

She stepped right down into the trench where I was and reached out her hand for mine, still singing. I stretched up into the sunlight of her face and felt the strands of her golden hair about my own. I closed my eyes for a second, knowing she had come to take me home, and when I opened them again my mouth was foul with mud, it was the middle of the night and the guns had started once more.

I remember one man saying to me: *we will never be able to see colour again*. We will never be able to see colour again. When I looked into his eyes I saw that there was nothing there, nothing left, and I felt afraid – I feared that I would be the same, that if I were to look into a mirror I would see the same blindness. But then I thought the fact that I was afraid of exactly that was proof something had survived after all! There was at least a candle flutter left that had not been extinguished.

There came a time we were on the move day and night. Of course we knew nothing, but I reckon things were bad: it must have been the winter of 1917. I was twenty years old and I felt seventy; it was as though birthday after birthday had been spent in this hell, that the years before were nothing but a dream. We were without sleep for four or five days. Once we had to take refuge in the shell of a house, knee-deep in mire, for a whole day. The ground around us shook and rumbled with explosions; the worst of it was you knew you were nothing more than a number in the most terrible game of roulette there ever had been. One man beside me went mad; he broke and fell and flailed about, sobbing uncontrollably, babbling gibberish. And the CO shot him, shot him in the head as though he was a dog. And he sank slowly; I remember watching him disappear into the darkness, his eyes still open, still full of unimaginable horror. And later, when we were still there, waiting for a lull in the shelling before we began crawling out over the bare ridge once more, yard by aching yard, I thought of the madness of it. That man had survived innumerable attacks, endless nights of bombardment by the enemy, to end up shot by one of his own. And I remember wanting to laugh; I can vividly remember standing in the stench of that foul mud and water, wanting to laugh at the sheer absurdity of it all. Yet I knew that if I broke out laughing I would be shot, because once I began it would be impossible for me to stop.

But the irony is that I survived; the dice did not roll for me. I think that for a time I believed I had made it, that I was going to be all right. I had passed the great shadow and now I was into the clear. It's the way children think when they're playing some game of hide and seek; it's no different from that. There's some core of us deep inside that remains the same despite all the adult armour we wear to disguise it. I would think of it when I first woke in the half-darkness and even smile to myself: *the worst is over, it is just a question of marking time.*

Where is everyone this morning? I don't understand what on earth is going on. Someone is usually here for me long before now; I only wish I could hear what was going on anywhere else in this place! It's still strange ringing a bell, pushing a button in the wall that's soundless to me, knowing someone else will hear and come. Perhaps that's what faith is.

I suppose it was three weeks later I was sent out with the night patrol. We were going to be moving again the following day, I'm pretty sure of that. It was so cold, so still. There was a glitter of stars but no moon. Even the muddied edge of the trench had frozen solid. We had to move so slowly, inch after inch drag ourselves over the ground in case snipers spotted us, picked us off one by one.

*

We were crossing the ridge when I was thrown backwards, my head exploding with the shell blast that ripped into the hillside. A hail of broken earth and broken men landed all around me. I landed on the bottom of the shell hole on my back, intact, except that I could hear nothing.

I was lucky they found me (at least that's what they said) and brought me back to the field hospital. They looked at me and saw a man unscathed: his fingers and toes, his limbs and his organs, his mind in one piece, almost. Was that not luck? Was that not amazing? To say you had lost your hearing sounded like a shrug of the shoulders, little more than losing a coin in the grass. I was lucky, and I was useless to them now.

So I went home and the war went on. But all the way back on trains and in stations filled with men heading the other way, streaming towards the last fading hope of breakthrough, I was locked into the silence of my own inner world. They wanted me to feel grateful because they could not see the thing I had lost, and the loss of that pearl of great price meant everything else became pale and strange and suddenly worthless. I even watched two men talking in sign language on the last train, their hands moving like rabbits in a moonlit field. I watched them until they saw me and stopped, staring at me, but I wanted to tell them, to shriek at them, that I was deaf and could not hear what they were saying.

At the end of the day it is the little things that always matter. I went back to my village; I walked down the same track I had left by all those years before, and they welcomed me – in silence. I could not hear my mother laughing as the new lamb came for its feed in the morning; I could not hear my father's axe as it thudded the wood for the stove. I could not hear the thatch of the dawn chorus, that net of song in the trees before the greyness lifted and morning began in earnest. And I could not hear Anna singing as she passed the house, the wild gold splayed about her shoulders, around the oval of her face and those blue, blue eyes.

So I left a second time. I ran away because I could not bear to hear that silence any longer, and because I could not bear to see the way Anna's eyes passed over me to the men who came home whole. At least she saw me as I was, disabled and different, bleeding inside from a wound that would never be healed again. I left one night because I could not bear to endure another morning unable to hear the singing of the birds.

Now I am old; I have everything and I have nothing. They look at me and they think: *what a miracle it was he survived those years of madness!* But they know nothing. I lie here alone in this Munich home, looking out south towards the first line of the German Alps, and I cannot hear the song of a robin as it comes in winter in hope of crumbs on a window ledge.

The Listener

It was in the Helsinki summer he realized he had to leave. They were working on the road at the back of the house. He understood for the first time in his life how men working at mending roads can only shout at one another. They laughed and shouted as the asphalt broke beneath their drills. He knew he had to go and listen. He felt as he had done many times before: a tugging urgency to be gone, to leave for somewhere he needed. Sometimes he was sure he had felt that way as a boy, but the truth was he didn't know. He *wanted* to believe it.

One night he spoke to Lars and told him he needed the cabin. His voice north of the Arctic Circle. In the window the sun breaking like an orange; the city rippling with heat. The traffic sighed in the streets: sleepless, restless, searching.

He stayed up packing until he heard only the house. He held his breath and listened and heard only the house's hum, and in the night's heat he slept.

*

The train was packed. They were leaving Helsinki for the weekend. Like a fool he'd chosen a Friday. Two women opposite chattered about everything necessary for a party, down to napkin rings and the colour of tablecloths. Children ran up and down, playing hide and seek. He tried to read and gave up; he tried to escape into the landscape that flickered past the windows, and he was drawn back and back to tables and chairs and placemats. And so he slept.

When he woke he realized he was alone. The train curling around a lake and sunlight playing in strings through the windows. They had slowed and as the train curled its wheels shrieked. They were in the north; they were heading north and all at once it surged through him. *Northern-ness*. His need of north had been there from the beginning, from the time of the first stories, the first forests. Harp strings of light played through the compartment, edged with orange so he knew it must be four or five o'clock. By nightfall he'd be there. A joy that might have been a child's surged through him and he found himself at the window opposite, peering into the light above the lake. A single wooden cabin in a clearing, its windows gold. This was where he was going, for as long as he needed, as long as it would take.

*

The seaplane nodded on the river. The blackfly were bad here by the water; a thick fur. But he knew. It was said you could always tell a stranger because they'd fight them off with their arms. The man walked six feet away from him: small, dark, quiet. There was no need to say anything but he wanted to say something nonetheless. They shared the same country yet inhabited different worlds. He was from Helsinki, even though the north was there on both sides of his family. This man was a Sámi, a Lapp. He'd made the journey with him to the cabin a dozen times and they'd never spoken; nothing beyond *Put your bag here*, or *This drum's the one to use*, or *That's the path over there*.

Once they'd left the ground it would have been impossible to talk anyway. Yet in the end the aircraft's song became something you grew used to, became another kind of silence. He'd thought the sun had set but he was wrong; it was there on the sky's edge – an orange ball lighting the lakes, just above the sea's rim. They must be a hundred miles beyond the Arctic Circle and this was still a world of bears and wolves. Something in the deepest core of him rejoiced, leapt. After their wars, after Auschwitz, after Chernobyl – a world that remained and lived.

They curled down to the lake, the engine suddenly all but gone. The silence held them. They curled like a white kite down and down to the water, skidding across the fierce blue. This was the beginning.

*

Before he did anything he cut wood. There was no need; Lars had stacked a month's worth of birch logs in the lee of the east wall. But he *had* to cut wood. The thud of the axe the only sound there was; it might have been carried all the way to Helsinki.

He cut wood until he shone, until he was breathless, and then he stopped. Pieces of pale yellow-white wood lay splintered all around his feet. There was a whisper of wind – no, not even so much as that. A *ghost* of wind; that was how he thought of it. You had to be exact with description; an approximation was not enough. That was true of words as much as of sounds. It was about listening and hearing exactness.

*

The second thing he did was to take out the paper he'd brought from Helsinki. He laid it under the window in the main room of the cabin. It caught the last light in the sky; became like sky itself – like pieces of sky.

The third thing he did was to look all around the cabin. It was turning dark now; everything falling under shadow. He stood at the door, opposite the window. The wood-burning stove to his right; the bunk beds to his left. A little further back the sink and what counted as a kitchen. The wooden floor. The lamp hanging from a hook in the middle of the ceiling. It was time to light the lamp. It was time.

*

He'd been christened on a day of thunderstorm when one of the city churches was struck by lightning. He'd never learned to drive a car. He'd been married twice: once he'd run away, the second time it was she who'd run from him. His father was still alive in an old people's home in Helsinki, transformed from a kind and forgiving man to an angry and incoherent one who threw things at nurses and recognized no one. His fame came and went in waves; he hadn't written anything proper for ten years. He'd been silent for almost ten years, but that did not mean he had been listening. He'd just been silent; hunched into himself and restlessly searching, moving through attics on the hunt for something that might not have been there to begin with.

It didn't grow dark that night. It shrank from yellow-blue to deep blue, the colour of a bruise. The stars that shone on the cloth of the sky were pale things, seed pearls weak as faint cries. You could have walked as far as morning carrying no light.

*

He found the lake by accident. He'd wandered from the cabin by a path that did not know where it was going until it opened into a clearing. The lake was black, almost perfectly round with dead trunks of trees sliding into it, like a mouth consuming wood – a strange reptile.

He went forward on soft feet and saw that he was wrong. The water wasn't black; it changed and shifted colour. A fish flickered the surface. At one end lilies whose white eyes were fading after their June lives. Sunlight danced in soft pools of brightness, even though the sun itself was hidden behind wreaths of cloud.

He went forward and looked at his reflection in the water. The dark accentuated the deep lines of his face; he was shocked by what he saw. The surface rippled with a cast of wind and his face was broken.

He crouched there until he lost all track of time. He did what the teachers in his Helsinki schools had punished him for – he daydreamed. But when he emerged from that inner world he saw himself with sudden clarity; as if with a scientist's sharp eye he stood beside himself, watching himself. He'd become part of nature, had gone back to nature. A beetle with a brown sheen crawled over the scuffed leather of his shoes. The frayed sunlight wove patterns on his left hand, flickered his cheek. And in his mind's eye he saw with sudden overwhelming clarity the flat in the city, silent and left behind.

*

He dreamed one night of the finding of a red gem, large as a cherry, its chambers glowing like a living heart. The most beautiful thing there was.

But then they came with machinery to dig away the forests and the mountains themselves, and he knew in the dream that it was in the hope of finding other stones. The landscape was changed beyond all recognition but they found nothing. There had been just one single gem.

He lay awake in the early morning, lying on his back in the pale hours before dawn. He lay and thought about how at times a dream could seem more real than waking. And he wondered too what it meant, what workings of his mind had come together to make this. For he had thought of no gem the day before, of no machinery or destruction. He did not know and he carried the fragments of it the whole day, lest he should understand.

*

There came a day he did not know what day it was. But then he realized he hadn't thought about days for far longer. If he couldn't remember today then he couldn't remember yesterday, nor the day before. He wanted to feel glad, like a child in summer who doesn't need to think about bells and uniforms and homework. He wanted to feel glad, yet in truth he knew he first felt fear. It was akin to sensing suddenly that you've swum far further than you imagined from the shore, that you're out of your depth. For a moment he felt afraid.

He left the cabin and took the path to the lake. He needed its sanctuary. It was a holding point, a certainty, in a landscape that bewildered and bewitched with its endless unchanging. It was a landscape impossible to learn, remember.

He came to the lake and there was a swan on its surface. He dropped involuntarily to his knees, became as low as he could in the grass and heather and dwarf birch. The swan was completely white. It might have been carved from ice; the only dark its eye. He realized it was rendered whiter by the deep black of the water, and he wondered just how white it would have seemed had he seen it against snow, had this been the middle of winter. Would it have been the snow that seemed white and not it at all?

He moved closer, almost noiselessly. The swan dipped the curl of its neck and its bill touched the water. Utter white against utter dark. It turned and began gliding towards him, close to where he'd crouched a few feet from the bank. It seemed to him the swan saw him, held his gaze and steered closer and closer. There was no fear there, neither was there curiosity. It was as though he had become part of that place, had crouched into it and his feet taken root.

He realized too he had no idea how long he'd crouched there watching. He'd lost all sense of time. And then he remembered how he'd woken that morning, afraid because he couldn't remember the name of the day – and all his fear flowed away. It was as he thought of it now that the fear left him and he felt liberated. He was freed into the joy of something else.

*

It was the coming of the wind that brought the sounds. He realized there had been no wind before then, nothing at all. The days hung still; each blade and leaf and stem held its breath, as though waiting and listening, like him.

One night he lay watching the stars. Nothing had moved all day; the trees sculpted from silence. The lake a single piece of black glass, untouched and unbroken. By the side of the path a fur of insects danced in stillness, a pillar of things in their own intricate tangling. For a moment he'd wanted to bring his bare hand into them, to know if they would brush against him or change their dance. But he didn't.

He lay and watched the stars. He could have walked through the night; it never went more than grey. The edges of the trees were there; the rims of the hills. But he didn't. He wanted to lie and listen to the stars. They flickered and fired on the grey cloth of the sky, and he thought how the dead ones drew him most – the ghosts of stars that were no more. They were the memories of stars and he was watching how once they were, and it made him wonder – as many times before – if it might be possible to travel until you could look back and see the earth as once it was.

He watched the crackling remnants of the stars until he thought they were like bonfires; like lonely bonfires in the sky, untended and desperately far from one another. He was pulled down into sleep and he walked that landscape, the vast distance between bonfires.

But he woke when he heard the wind – long, slow casts about the cabin. The wind was unhurried; a great, slow searching. He heard too the dried and empty fragments of heather, the tiny pieces of dwarf birch, gathered and carried in the wind's hands.

He got up, naked, in the early morning nothingness of the day, and watched and listened.

He stood there and in front of the window, underneath it, were all the sheets he'd brought to fill, bare and blank after however many days of being, of listening. And at that moment the wind blew, fierce and real, and broke the membrane that had lain for ten years over his hearing, and the sounds came, the notes came. And he scrambled for a pencil as they poured out of the grey gusts that early morning; he knelt naked, shivering and mad, as they came and he caught them at last.

There was a flickering of things before his eyes: the swan on the lake, the trees, the dream of the red gem, the light on the cottage windows, the seaplane and the white curl out of the sky. He found what they were themselves but he fought for what joined them and made them one. It was the little turning points of sound that he sought and he lay there, listening, straining to hear, until he caught them, one after another. He stayed there until the last one was found. He was freezing cold on the cabin floor and the pages lay scattered about him, in pieces. They were fragments that had come at random, but they were all there, waiting. The notes had come.

A Christmas Child

I t was a clear, frost-sharp night in the middle of November. Rachel had banked the fire; the thick smell of mutton soup filled the house. Perhaps it was that that had cheered Angus; he had had no luck with the fishing, came home dispirited and worried after five days at sea. And because he had had no luck, neither had anyone in the village. This was the worst time in the year; this was the hardest of it.

On such days Angus had to break driftwood, even when it left splinters in his hands. He needed the crisp snap of wood from the store; it was good to come in with a bundle in his arms and afterwards see the curl of orange flames in the grate. Now it was peat that lay dark at the back of the fire; his eyes dreamed in the wreaths of smoke.

There was a soft knock at the door. Who at this hour? When he opened, he could just see the shadow of the figure outside.

'We're going down to the point tonight, to try our luck with bringing in a ship. Will you come?'

He heard the pause between the first and second sentences. He heard his heart too, racing far harder than usual. Not only because of the lack of fish that day.

'I've told you before, Donald John, I'll have nothing to do with it. Do you and your boys not listen? I'll have no part in your business.'

The shadow moved in the doorway but did not turn away. 'Then you'll have no part in the shares either.'

Not a threat, a statement. One man left; the other closed his door. He said not a word to Rachel. They went to bed an hour later, heard nothing of the calls and deliberations out on the road at midnight. There was a soft fall of hail about one; afterwards there was not a thing to be seen or heard. The cries had been drowned; the lanterns had disappeared. There was just the endless sea, combing the rocks, boom after long boom.

The following day was beautiful. There wasn't a breath of wind. The low sun hung white in the skies and the last rowans trembled on a bough on the tree at the road end. Angus left before first light; crept out of bed and padded down the stairs, his satchel over his left shoulder. He was going into town for this and that, though there was precious little to spend. Rachel heard the soft thud of the door, then turned and slept once more.

*

She was washing clothes in the house when the knock came, urgent. She called that she would come in a moment; she carried the steaming pot of water to the stone flags, sighing. She wanted the clothes to be done by the time Angus came back.

She opened the door as the shadow of a girl fled. A call faded on her lips. There was a boy on the doorstep; a boy with brown eyes like hazelnuts and tight dark curls. She bent down at once beside him and she was still taller than the little soul. His eyes searched her, wide and unblinking.

'And where did you come from?' she breathed. 'Where in the world did you come from?'

It had been the best haul in many years. When Angus came back through the village they were still dividing out sacks and boxes. There was the scent of rich tobacco in the air. Robert and Cam were roaring with laughter at something; as Robert's face turned at Angus' approach the smile died on his face. It changed slowly, became at last a sourness, a sneer. The faces said nothing as he passed, yet they said everything.

He did not go into the house then, but carried on instead to the shore. It was high tide. The vessel was out on the rocks; a small thing of dark boards and ropes, crumpled and useless. All at once he remembered a boy in school who had once taken a huge spider between his fingers and crushed it. He had smiled and looked around him, hoping the others would see, approve. Angus felt now as he had then; he felt no different.

He went as far as he could in the direction of the wreck. The tide was fierce; he was not fool enough to venture further. And there among the dark boards he saw one single white hand. It did not even cross his mind for a moment that the hand belonged to a living soul; the sea was like ice and this was mid-November. All he did was to pull away the cap from his head and close his eyes, mutter some words he would have been too shy to speak aloud in front of Rachel, and turn away to the house.

As soon as he came inside, she took his hand and led him upstairs, one finger pressed to her lips. The boy slept, more like a doll than a child, so quiet it was hard to know he breathed. She told Angus in a single flutter of words how he had come to the house.

'I understand,' he said, understanding indeed.

Over the next weeks he seemed to do nothing but work. The days were fine – bitterly cold but beautiful. A few flakes of snow came to the island hills, made them look like the wing of a bird. The snow lay in the heather, would lie there for the whole winter.

He mended the roof of the house, his hands raw and cut with the cold. The salt from the sea was in that wind. All day he worked, until the sun went down like a ball of snow in the west.

Jacob came out to look up at him. Rachel held his hand, and the brown eyes looked up at him – both pairs of eyes looked up at him. Angus tried to think of something to say but he could think of nothing. He smiled too and it hurt to smile; even that hurt. They had called him Jacob after her grandfather.

One day he was down again at the shore and he found a sea urchin. It was no bigger than his thumbnail. He carried it home as he might have carried a fledgling fallen from the nest.

'Close your eyes, Jacob,' he whispered. He opened the little hand and laid the shell on it. 'Happy Christmas,' he said, and kissed the nut-brown smoothness of his forehead.

Later that day he knew there was something that had to be done.

'I want you to come with me,' he said to Rachel. 'I want both of you to come with me.'

They wrapped up warm against the wind and went out and closed the door behind them. It was still beautiful; the skies a winter blue, the white waves chasing in over the rocks. They went up to the village, up towards the happy laughter of the village street and a man with a squeezebox. Four of the girls were dancing; the men were laughing. They walked through the village street and the music fell away to nothing, the heads hung down, the eyes looked away. Donald John was turning back into his house. Angus carried the child in his arms; he held Rachel's hand as he walked.

He stopped and smiled and gently put the child down in front of him.

'Donald John,' he said softly, 'you gave us a share after all.'

Out

It was the Friday afternoon when Ranald punched his brother. Angus had made a comment about Kirsty, who had been Ranald's sweetheart for almost a year now, and it was not the kind of comment any man would have wanted to hear about the girl he loved. Ranald's punch had split his brother's nose there in the barn that evening; he didn't stay to see what damage had been done, he simply turned on his heel and walked down into the field, his hand still sore from the blow.

It so happened that one of the old men was going out with the lobster pots and would drop into Mallaig on the way back. Ranald asked if he could join him for the ride and Donald Gorrie didn't even nod his reply. He looked up towards the Sgurr of Eigg and they were off. Without asking or being told, Ranald dropped lobster pots as they went; there was nothing to talk about so they said nothing, and Donald Gorrie kept his eye on the water, thinking about his sister in hospital and the eggs he had to pick up from the croft before he went to bed that night.

*

Ranald jumped off in Mallaig and his hand still hurt. The only thing alive in Mallaig was an articulated lorry with its engine chugging, the men loading up lobsters and crabs for tables in the south of Spain. Ranald asked the driver if he could have a lift and the man, who had a face like a living walnut, thought about it a long time. In the end he said yes as though he had taken a decision of immense magnitude, and half an hour later they roared away into the June night.

It was beautiful and Ranald wished he could have told the driver the names for islands and the stories of infamous fishing trips. He told them again to himself as the sky went a deep blue and the stars filled it like brine. The last thing he remembered before he drifted off to sleep was that his hand still hurt. It was like guilt except he felt none, and his sleep was easy and untroubled.

He left the articulated lorry when they reached Finisterre. The driver had given him some long story in Spanish which Ranald had guessed was all about how his boss would fire him for having a passenger and that it would be best for him to get off now. Ranald had bought him a beer in Nantes with some cents he had kept in the back pocket of his jeans for almost two years. He clapped the driver on the shoulder and thanked him, and went off into Finisterre.

*

The ship that he found in port bound for South America was involved in some kind of wicked business. He knew that as soon as he went on board. There was a bad smell about the vessel, in every sense. They didn't care where he came from nor where he wanted to go; a very camp man called Alberto showed him the containers that had to be stacked and weighed. He would be paid in dollars and he'd have to share a cabin with three others. Ranald said yes to everything.

He had been on the sea before, fishing out of Peterhead when he was seventeen. He had earned so much money he could hardly walk to the bus when he came ashore, his wallet was that heavy. He hadn't been sick once, though he'd felt queer early one morning after a full breakfast on the way back to port.

The sea got to him now on the fifth day out, but it was as much the ship as the sea. There was the smell below deck you never got away from, and the cabin stank of that and sweat and something else. He was sick and it was bile that came up in the end. He had a raging thirst and there was no one to ask to bring him water. He couldn't stop thinking about Kirsty, missing her and wishing he had never left. He tried to sleep and he couldn't, and the relentless sea went down and up and down.

*

When he woke in the night two of the men were playing a game of chess. His mouth was cracked and sore; it hurt even to open it. In his mind they were playing their game with the devil.

If they won, everything would be all right, but if they didn't Ranald would be thrown into the sea. And then he sank into a shallow sleep where he seemed to be arguing with the devil, but it was all about weights and measures, and what could be bought and sold. Later he woke and knew that he had to drink; his body told him that if he didn't he would die. Somehow he got up, as though in a dream, with moonlight swaying through the cabin, and he found his way to the toilet where he was sick until there was nothing left. Then he drank and drank and washed his face, and when he looked in the mirror he saw his brother's eyes looking back at him. But he felt better and he slept until the following day.

He had no idea where he was when he landed except that he was somewhere in Brazil. The girl he spoke to in the shop told him the name in such a beautiful voice that for a moment he forgot Kirsty and wanted to ask her to take him home, to let him lie down and eat fruit and laugh again. But he didn't because he couldn't; it wasn't possible to do things like that, and he just smiled at her green eyes and went out to the pavement in the brilliant sunlight that somehow was brighter than anything he'd seen before.

How he got a ride with a man who sold hammers and spare parts for motorbikes he never really worked out. But it was enough to be heading towards the capital with the windows open and the wind in his face, listening to happy music the driver sang to all the way there. The man bought him a beer at a roadside café, and Ranald told him that if he ever made it as far as his island he would have all the lobsters he wanted and a girl called Katie Ann. The man laughed and put his arm round Ranald's shoulder, and after the beer Ranald really meant it – he hoped the man would land up on his island one day! He left his mobile number on an old serviette and they drove on, into the night.

But in Brasilia a huge loneliness gripped him, a homesickness that almost made him cry. He was going home the whole time, after a day's fishing, after mending a tractor on the other side of the island, after being with his cousins at Torbeg. He was always coming home.

He counted the coins in his pocket, changed his money, and took a taxi out to the airport. At a desk he asked the price of a ticket to London. He had less than a tenth of what he needed. He didn't even have the money for the taxi back; he walked a long way and then took the bus. What came to him was the story of the prodigal son; that was what he thought of in the dry silence of the afternoon at the bus stop. The air was full of insects; the sounds of dry insects.

He found a job in an Irish bar and it took him a long month. He ate like a mouse, saved the smallest coins for new meals. He prayed for tips. The owner of the bar was a man who had no idea where Ireland was, but one of the bartenders had an aunt who seemed to be distantly related to someone from Kilkenny. Everyone talked English, and everyone thought Ranald came from Ireland. In the end he told people that he did; it seemed to bring him more in the way of tips.

Then came a Thursday when he could go out to the airport and buy his ticket. It felt as though he had won the lottery. Something sang in the left side of his chest. And then it dawned on him: he had no passport. His passport was in his father's desk, in the top left-hand corner of the upper shelf. He thought of phoning Angus to ask him to post it, but that was a matter of pride. He didn't want to ask any favours of Angus. Instead he found the British Embassy and spoke to a man called Peter Constantine who furnished him with the necessary papers after an interminable conversation with the authorities in London. Ranald heard every heartbeat in his chest as the conversation went on in an office beyond the desk; he made out some of the words but not all of them. The following day he picked up papers that had been sent by email from the office in London; Ranald thanked Peter Constantine too profusely and afterwards felt embarrassed. He closed the door of the Embassy behind him with gratitude and a deep breath. He was going home.

There was one person from the island he knew was in London. He phoned Davie Macdonald from a call box and got the fellow's mobile number, and late that afternoon he tracked him down. They met for a pint and Ranald was welcome to stay over; it was a case of a couch and a spare toothbrush.

They talked about the landing of a famous fish and he drank too much whisky, but he felt London around him like some gigantic beast. He was trapped right in its heart and he slept fitfully, too hot and restless until the morning. At the breakfast table the older man slapped some notes into his hand, told him it was enough for the train as far as Edinburgh. No, no – he would get it back some time; that was what being neighbours was all about.

At the station he got his ticket and by lunchtime he was onto the train. What was that about a Scot loving the last few feet of the King's Cross platform more than anything else in England? The train curled north: Peterborough, Doncaster, Leeds, Durham, Newcastle, Edinburgh. And the air was fresh when he got out at the platform; the sound of gulls raucous about him in windy blue sky.

He had just enough for the last ticket, but nothing for a meal. He drank all the water he could at the gents, then boarded the train. Three hours and he felt every moment; he never forgot rounding that bend and seeing the sea for the first time. He felt like a prisoner released after twenty years.

Fortunately it was the cousin of Donald Black who was skippering the ferry that evening, and he walked on for free. He had to go up to the wheelhouse for the half-hour, but he said never a word about where he had been.

He stepped ashore and wouldn't take a lift from Jimmy the Post. He'd tell his own story in his own time; he didn't need Jimmy's help with that. And it came to him as he pushed the yards behind him going up the track he had no idea what day or even what month it was, or how long he'd been away. There at the top of the road was Kirsty, a couple of letters to post in her hand, as though she might have been waiting for him all that time. And her mouth was open with a question she never uttered; he didn't stop but kissed her, and there was something in that kiss that meant more, that wasn't to be misunderstood.

He went on up to the farmhouse and in at the back door, and he heard the television's voice in the living room. He went in and thumped down on the other side of the sofa, and Angus half-turned to look at him. Ranald kept his eyes on the screen.

'Where've you been?' Angus asked.

Ranald thought a moment.

'Out,' he said.

The Gift

I know what it was I wanted to tell you about, it was Christmas. I call myself a traveller who never did, but my mother and father were both brought up on the road. It was my mother who wanted to settle, long before I was born. She'd lost my older brother to pneumonia. They'd been out in the west with the horse and cart one October, in a storm that lasted for days. Everything was drenched and frozen in the end and my brother died before they could get help for him. I think that was why they came to Dublin. I think that was it.

Well, I remember one year I was at school – I would have been six at the time. And the teacher was a Miss Munro, she was a spiteful woman. She was no taller than a pencil and the boys trembled in front of her. She should have been out breaking horses, not in a classroom breaking the spirits of children. She knew fine the names they called me and she was deaf to all of them. If she could find a way to punish me she would. I was forever going off into my own world. I'd sit there with my head on my arm looking out into the school playground. There was one tree there, a cherry, and I loved just looking at its blossom in the spring and listening to the leaves. One morning Miss Munro must have caught me staring away at that tree and she came charging up the row, twisting my ear in her fingers until she'd hauled me onto my feet, shouting over and over –

'Are you away with the fairies, Mary Riley? Are you away with the fairies?'

It was coming near Christmas and I'd seen my father pacing again at home.

'The wolf in him wants out,' my mother whispered to me as she put a button onto a shirt. But there was the ghost of a smile on her mouth as she spoke the words, and I saw her glance at him as she spoke, though he never turned, only kept pacing.

This particular day Miss Munro had shouted at me for my shoes, the state of my shoes. I felt so small and embarrassed there in the class, and I could hear the sniggers around me; I could tell the rest of them relished my suffering. By breaktime my face was smudged with crying and I felt broken in bits. And suddenly my father was there, in the corridor, and I remember he just picked me up in his arms as if I'd been a bale of hay or a young calf. It wasn't the end of the school day and Miss Munro came charging out of her classroom.

'Do you people not know what time is?' she screamed shrilly, and her red mouth seemed the only thing in her small, white face. 'Do you people have no idea what time is?'

My father laughed. I could feel his laugh as he held me, but it wasn't a bitter or an angry laugh; it was soft and just edged with a lace of mockery, no more than that.

'Ah, you know what clocks are, but we know what time is.'

And with that he turned and went, carrying me still in his arms, as though he was bearing me from a burning building. And all the shrieking of Miss Munro at his back was as grass blowing in the wind to him.

And out there was my father's old van, and I was puzzled, for he never came to collect me from school. I always made the journey myself, even though it was a long walk on a winter morning.

'Where are we going, Dad?' I asked him as he put me into the car, and it was warm and I caught the smell of him, from his hair perhaps.

'We're going on a journey, Moorie,' he said softly, and I knew then he was in a really good mood. If he was sad he drank, and then sometimes he wouldn't speak to my mother or me for days, but just stare from the second-floor window, away towards the hills, as though he wasn't there at all. But when he was happy he ruffled my hair and his brown eyes shone like river stones and he called me Moorie.

We're going on a journey.

And everything was in the back of his van, and my whole heart filled with excitement. I'd been off with him and my mother in the summertime, to camp by rivers and in glens, to listen to traveller stories at night by the fire. But I'd never been away in winter, when we were stuck in the city, in the fog and the freezing rain. Now we were going on a journey.

What I remember is that night. He was looking for somewhere, my father. We were nearly there, wherever *there* was. And I was in the back, lying among blankets and coats because he was afraid I'd get cold. And I remember looking out and seeing all those stars. There was a jeweller's in Dublin that had diamonds in the window set on a black velvet cloth. And that was what I thought of now as we bumped and rattled along back roads in search of the place my father wanted to find.

And some of me wanted to be there, to know what the place was, and some of me never wanted to be there at all. I wanted to stay where I was for ever, looking up at the stars as the van lurched and hummed on and on into the dark.

But at last we juddered to a halt and the silence flooded back. I had no idea what time it was and my father set up the simple tent between two trees. There was no sound in all the world and there was a frost; it was as though a giant in one of the stories of Old Ireland had breathed over everything – the trees, the fields, the hills – and turned them to a silver mist.

*

And my father taught me how to make a fire. He taught me that kindling is everything, that it's the little pieces that matter. The big bits of wood are all very well, they count later on, but there's no fire to begin with if there's no kindling. And he said it was just like that with the travellers, that the big people – the doctors and the teachers and the judges – they were all very well, but they would be nowhere without the little people, the ones who pulled the carts and cleared the fields and mended the roads.

My hands were so cold as I found pieces of wood and kindling and brought them to my father. But when I came back the second time he had lit the fire and was blowing on it, blowing so the flames roared, and I thought to myself that he was a kind of dragon, a magical creature that could do anything in the world he wanted.

I crouched beside that fire and stretched out my hands to it. I felt the orange glow warm on my cheeks. And my father told me about how the travellers came to be, all that time ago in Jerusalem when Jesus was alive. For they had come looking for someone who would make the nails for Jesus' cross, and no one would do such a thing, for he had been full of only goodness and kindness all his days. But the traveller said he would, and he lit his fire and flapped it into life with his apron. And ever since the traveller has been on the move, restless, journeying from place to place, the ghost of the nails he made shadows in every fire he makes. And I looked for the ghosts of the nails but I couldn't see them.

And I went to bed with the words still circling my head like stars, and I wondered what we were, we travellers; were we good or were we bad? Was I ashamed to be one for the sin of that first traveller, or was I glad that we were different, that we had learned to find our way in the world by different paths, by secret roads? And I dreamed that night that I was lost, and went knocking and knocking on door after door. But no one would tell me and no one would help me, and everyone just sent me on my way once more.

He woke me first thing next morning.

'Come on, Moorie,' he said, and I knew this was it, that now at last I was going to find out why he had brought me here.

We walked into the forest, and it was what he always called a foxy wood. It was dark; the trunks were close and branches snapped underfoot. It smelled of owls and moss and green things. But there was a path, a ribbon of a thing that wound its way between stumps and vanished in a pale thread.

'The travellers have been coming here for a thousand years, Moorie,' he whispered, and I didn't know why he whispered, but my heart fluttered like a bird in my chest and I drank in the place with all of my senses.

*

And at last we came to a glade, a round clearing in the woods, and I looked up at the branches and in them were the strangest globes. I thought at first they were hives – that was what came to me to begin with, that they were wild hives of bees. Some of them were only small and others were big as the globe of the world the headmaster had in his room back in Dublin.

'Mistletoe!' my father hissed. 'Mistletoe, Moorie! And it's been grown here by the travellers, because it has to be grafted!' And he explained to me about grafting, and about what mistletoe was. And it seemed to me it was magical, this strange thing growing in globes above my head, with its white berry that was like a river pearl, a cloudy white.

All day we picked mistletoe there in the glade. My father climbed the trees and cut little pieces and dropped them. It was my job to run here and there, collecting them from where they fell, and gather them into bundle after bundle after bundle.

And when we left in the end and drove to a nearby town we sold mistletoe at all the houses, pieces for a few pence. It was frosty and our breath fluttered about us like scarves, and my father told me stories and taught me songs. He was so different from the way I knew him at home in the council estate, among the dogs and the rubbish and the drink. Here he was different: he was himself.

That night the rain came and a kind farmer offered us his barn to sleep in. My father wouldn't have me getting soaked; he had a horror of that after my brother's death. The barn was warm with a thick smell; we made our beds and listened to the rain on the roof above us. And the rain was like songs too. And in the night I dreamed that this was the place where Jesus had been born. I had come too in order to see this newborn king. But everyone had presents with them, the shepherds and the kings – I was just a traveller and I had nothing. But then I looked at my hand and I saw there was a sprig of mistletoe – the last one that hadn't been sold – and I went to the manger and held it above the baby's head and I kissed him.

That's what I wanted to tell you. The story of the best Christmas I've ever known.

The Healing

The old man looked at him wearily in the half-dark of the stone cell. He had been up since five that morning, and the ache in his left hip had not lessened in the least. But still he did not allow himself to sit to pray. Now it was almost ten and he ached to lie down, to stretch out and let sleep carry him away. Had he battled against such things as this for fifty years with such futility?

'I am asking if I can go to the island.'

The young man was only a shadow in front of him. He stood and did not move, and did not know what it meant to be sore and old. Silence lay between them and as a paw of wind came and caught the tower so it shuddered; they heard the pattering of snowflakes against the glass. The track would be buried by morning, and the last of the wood was still to be brought in.

Only eight were ever chosen each December, and six of those were there year on year: they did not ask if they might have a place. His hip throbbed so he wanted to weep; a dull, deep drumbeat. The candle fluttered and he found himself nodding, though he did not look at the boy.

'Why do you want to go?'

He tried to keep the question steady and was not sure he had managed. The boy was seventeen; once he too had been seventeen and sure of nothing but the knowledge the sun would rise the next day. He looked through the gloom to find the boy's face. If there had been no kindness in his question then may there be some in his eyes.

'My sister.'

Just a whisper, and the young head bowed and shuddered. The boy wept. It took the old man by surprise, caught him almost like that breath of wind and knocked him softly sideways. He did not know what to do or say. He waited and heard his own heart. He watched and waited.

'All right,' he said in the end, quietly, hearing the strangeness of his own words. 'You may go.'

*

The chapel on the island belonged to St Lucy. It had been hers since the days she lived herself (leastways that was what the farrier would have said, had you disturbed him at his labour on a good day and he had the time to answer). The chapel belonged to St Lucy, and the legend was that she went there herself, however many hundred years back into the darkness of time. A family lived on the island; survived on what little they grew and on the sweet fish from the lake. The youngest girl fell ill with fever (local people still maintained it was at harvest, for the father was gone to help in the mainland fields, though how anyone knew *that* was a wonder). But word went out of the girl's fever, that she was sick unto death and nothing more could be done for her. In those days children were like apples from a tree; carry a bunch in your arms and you could be sure one or more would fall. But word went out of the girl's illness, and perhaps with the father himself as he went to gather the harvest. For that part of Russia was a land of fields, and whether the seas went dry or the wind stopped blowing, the fields must be delivered of their harvest.

So it was Lucy herself heard of the girl's dying, and came to the village as night was falling. (The farrier would tell you how many generations ago that was, for his family had been there since Eve put them all out of Eden.) But the boatman wouldn't go near the lake; there was no moon that night and all manner of stories of beasts that lived in the deep. The truth was he probably feared the fever himself, had no wish to bring it back to five sons and a wife.

So she walked. Lucy left the ferryman's house, went into the moonless night and down to the shore and walked. Even now the farrier will tell you there were three that stood and watched as she started onto the water as if it was no more than a dry path. And they say she walked barefoot, shoes in her hand; that her mouth moved and she prayed as she went. All the way to the other side and the island shore.

She went to the house where the girl lay in the last throes of fever, babbling words of nonsense. And Lucy's hand smoothed her forehead and she spoke soft words over and over, like the dripping of cool water, till at last the girl was still. But she was not dead, she slept.

*

The boy had been the third son. He had almost not survived, came into the world like a bundle of lamb that slips into the sleet-white grass with the tiniest cry. Born a month early and it was his sister who watched over him until at last he was stronger and the flags of the daffodils blew triumphant in the spring wind. Only five she was and she watched over him, for their mother could do nothing that first month, so ravaged was she from the long birth. That set a bond between them for ever, a bond that ran deep and strong. He was often ill in those first years. He struggled to breathe, to climb the hill of each new-drawn breath. It was she who sat with him through the long hours of the night, drawing the forefinger of her left hand across his cheek, slow and gentle, whispering the name she'd given him.

She would not let him be scolded. When the birch rod was raised by a mother half-mad with tiredness in a house with too many children, the girl shrieked and implored her to stop. That only maddened the mother the more, and set her against the girl. In summer the two escaped into the hills behind the house like leverets, laughing; the tin pails they carried for berries clanking against their thighs as they ran.

Their mother called them outlaws; she carried the washing out shouting at them still though they were far beyond hearing. They came back home, barefoot and weary, when the moon was orange in the river and the windless skies were all but dark. There was no point raising the birch rod then; she knew it was far too late.

Was she punishing the boy by sending him to the monastery or thanking God for the miracle of his birth? By that time his sister had gone to work as a servant at the big house of the landowners from Petersburg. She did not want to go, but there was no choice, and she sent home one silver coin every second week to her mother, despite all the years of the birch rod. The boy found the world strange without her, and in those first days he struggled to sleep at all. He said nothing aloud; did everything he was asked as always. But her absence was in his face, and nothing his mother said could hide it. When he went to the monastery he knew he was travelling in the opposite direction; he felt his sister growing distant behind him, though it was dark and starless and the road twisted many times. It was she he missed, not his mother.

*

It was when he was out by the well that he knew she was ill. The wind rushed through the autumn trees and he thought of them running in the thrill of it as once they'd done, and as he dipped his bucket into the stars on the surface he knew she was ill. Not just that she was ill but that it was something on her right side, and he touched the place with his free hand as he set the pail down with its shining.

He knew he should pray for the world, for its suffering, but he prayed for it somehow through her. When he knelt and words poured through him like a wild stream's babble it was her face he saw beyond him. He even prayed something of his strength might be given to her, that he might give it back all these years later.

And so he was told he could go to the island. As if by magic, the days froze and the eye of the lake glazed a strange white. He heard the ice crystals in the trees at night, the high song of them playing in the darkness. The sun climbed into the sky but it was a snowball, weak enough to look at full. And there were wolves; somewhere in the hills their voices held and echoed. He thought of them as the living sound of the northern lights; he told no one yet that was what he thought.

She was weakening. She had fallen and was weakening but he was kind to her. Those were the words he woke with, one morning when he rose and went to the window and six slow geese beat a path into the light. It was only six days till St Lucy's Day, until they went to the island.

*

And so they walked across the ice. They held their shoes, in memory of St Lucy, and walked in bare feet. At first the pain was almost too much to bear, until he realized that he felt nothing at all. He looked at his feet and thought they were like marble, and remembered the one time he visited the Winter Palace and saw the sculpture of the angel.

The men who walked with him now were old. He felt that as they walked they carried not only their shoes but their stories. They had lived through the story of Russia and grown old, and knew now that this was the last time they might visit the chapel. They wore white robes and they were the only things in the night's darkness, and the only sound that of their feet and their breathing. They did not talk; they looked ahead towards an island they could not see, and that itself was a kind of metaphor. The chapel must be in darkness when they came to it; as though they could not even be sure as they crossed it was there at all. Light and fire were only to be found and made later, once they had reached the other side.

He knew somehow that he loved them even now, those men, although he had been with them only days. He did not understand the meaning of years as they did. The one who fed the birds at dawn, who held fragments of bread in his cupped hand until they came and ate without fear. The one who was all but blind, but who sang in the morning with a voice as sweet as a child's. The one who did not talk any more, who had gone so far into silence words were not needed now. He had found a place where there was no more fear or anger.

That night the moon did not shine. There were stars, yet not as he had seen them before. Now they were like breath across the sky; a mist far beyond counting. The monks did not look back as they walked; that was also a part of their pilgrimage. And the ice was strange and patterned; he thought of the northern lights, and it was as if they had been imprisoned there, a moment of their fire frozen for ever.

It was only when they reached the other side he knew how cold it was.

*

Two days later, when they had returned to the monastery, he woke from a dream and knew he must go. He dressed in the dark, hands trembling, and fled down the stone steps as though the dream had not ended at all. It did not even occur to him to ask if he could leave.

It had snowed in the night and the silence left behind was bigger almost than silence itself. When the spines of dawn came, it was as though a bonfire burned somewhere ahead of him; a conflagration setting fire to the trees. When the sun had all but risen into the woods, its brightness was so great his eyes could not bear it. But he knew he was walking the right way; he knew he must walk into the sun.

He had no sense of time. He had walked countless miles with her all those years of his childhood; they had not known what time meant. For hours now he walked straight on; no path except the one his feet found. But he knew he was right; he knew without a shadow of a doubt, there was no other way but this. He came at last to the road; looked left and right and listened. He held his breath and heard the rustling of birds in the trees. Everything was dry; made of tinder-dry fragments.

He turned left and knew now he was not far away. And it was only then he seemed to waken and wonder what they would think and where he had gone. Then he saw a house and forgot everything as he began walking again. He could not walk but had to run, so hard his chest seemed burning and about to burst. He staggered on because he knew it was there, that she was there, that he must get there. And a beautiful garden and a long drive and the scent of woodsmoke and at last, after however many hours, a doorway and his fist on the hard wood, hammering and hammering and hammering.

She answered, for she was a servant there. And her face smiled, even though she cried.

'Sasha,' she said. 'I knew you would come.'

The Miracle

It had been a long night. Rangers had thrashed Celtic the day before. The whole of Glasgow had echoed with shouted songs and smashed windows. The last goings home at four in the morning. And the morning itself grey and ragged as if the city was hung over. The distant rattle of a train. A newspaper unfolded itself and blew into pieces on the edge of a wind that came and went.

Sonia Macpherson walked, her collar up against the cold and her hands buried in her pockets. She might have been the only one alive. She could have been still in bed; it was a Sunday morning, for God's sake! But she had to go and see Marie. It was two weeks since she'd managed to go and see her last. No, that wasn't quite true. She hadn't been able to face it. Sometimes it was just too much going in there. It stayed with you, the memory of the place – the memory of Marie.

*

Marie O'Brien, a wee Irish woman who lived three flights up a tenement in Ibrox. How on earth had she ended up in Ibrox, in that bit of Glasgow that was home to Rangers Football Club, that had only hatred for Catholic Ireland and all it had brought with it?

The Miracle

For thirty years they had thundered on Marie's door and stuffed every piece of filth they could find through her letterbox. Her name on the door was enough for that.

Now she was dying; she'd been dying for a long time. Some people went in a second, others slid away inch by inch. Sonia started up the steps, the only noise the scuffing of her feet on the stone. Somewhere a door boomed; no voices, just a smell. It was that that haunted her; she felt it in the pit of her stomach, had to force herself to keep going. Everything was in that smell.

She rattled the key in the lock and went in, thudded the door behind her. She started speaking Marie's name at once, her voice soft – almost songlike. She went through into the bedroom and swept back the curtains, still speaking her name, not expecting any answer, as much to comfort herself as anything else. It was fear in a way – that was it, fear of all this and fear of what she might find.

She turned round. Marie was curled away in the bed, curved into the clothes. There was nothing of her. She made noises to herself that were pieces of words, the memories of words. Sonia went over and brought her up against the pillow. She felt breakable; she had the frame of a bird, her bones brittle, her arms spindles. As she brought her up Sonia spoke in a bright voice all the time, about the weather and the cold days there had been in England, about her friend Janette who was off in Portugal. Then she looked up and caught the face of Ciaran, his picture on the bedside table, the picture of his smile. Ciaran, Marie's only son, who hadn't come to visit in years. When Sonia started coming, however long ago that was, Marie had never stopped talking about him. How he had a fancy house in England and was going to take her there – a fancy house with a garden and a stream. But he never came and gradually Marie stopped talking about him and Sonia didn't ask. The talk had faded like the picture.

She glanced behind the picture at a card, an Easter card. The picture of a grinning rabbit with huge teeth, gold and shining. All at once she remembered this was Easter, Easter Sunday.

'Happy Easter, Marie!' she said, turning round to crouch beside the bed. The eyes were there, just and no more – fragments of faded blue. Sonia nearly asked her how she was and then stopped. What was the point? Did Marie even know her now? She caught that smell again and felt sick. She ought to be gone, out of this place and away. She wanted to forget every last thing about it; she wished she wouldn't ever have to come back. There was a sudden thundering on the outer door and she jumped, was torn out of her thoughts. Expletives and a thud and a group of young men thudding down the stairs laughing. How had Marie survived thirty years of this place?

And it was that that made her see her again, made her remember why she had come. She looked at the tiny face.

'Is there anything I can get you, Marie? Anything you'd like?'

She was whispering something now, her voice thin as paper.

Sonia bent to hear; she all but had her ear against her mouth. 'A service?'

She tried to think what she meant. What service? Again the dry fragments of a word on the old woman's lips; again Sonia had to come as close as she could to make it out.

'Oh, the radio – a service on the radio!'

The ghost of a smile. The memory of a smile. The blue eyes kindled.

'Where is the radio, Marie?'

She couldn't keep that edge of annoyance out of her voice as she got up again. Marie's eyes had glazed: she had no idea. Where in all this mess was there a radio? Sonia moved cushions and blankets, unearthed a pair of scissors, coins and crumbs. She didn't want to do this. She wanted to be gone. It was Easter Sunday and it was a holiday; she could take a bus up to Loch Lomond and be as far away from this as it was possible to get.

There was the radio; it must have fallen behind the sofa from the window ledge. She looked back at Marie and she saw her again, her head bent forwards as though she was drifting into sleep once more. What she needed was a priest, not a radio. But how many priests were there in Ibrox? It almost sounded like the first line of a joke.

She clicked the dial of the ancient box and there was nothing. Not even that hiss that meant there might be something. It was dead. It was just an empty box that might have lain forgotten behind the sofa for years.

'Marie, pet, I'll go and make you a cup of tea.'

She put the radio into the old woman's hands tenderly. At least she had found what she'd asked for. In the kitchen she looked out of the window onto the city morning. How was it all the colours seemed to go in winter? It was as if they were washed into the Clyde and lost. Slate grey rain over slate grey hills over slate grey Glasgow. There was a movement on the tiny concrete window ledge. A robin; not a robin with its puffed-out red chest, the Santa Claus robin of Christmas cards, but a thin robin – a spindly thing that was still bright-eyed, with a breast that wasn't orange but more the colour of dark blood. Yet it stood out all the same, against all that was dead.

She stirred the tea for Marie: milk and sugar. The sweetness of it rose to her face. At least that was something she could give her. She'd done that and she could go with a clear conscience. The carers would be coming in at ten.

She turned to go back through to the bedroom. As she got to the doorway she saw everything; Marie in the middle of it all. The old woman hadn't moved; the radio was clutched in her hands just as it had been, the curtains were open, the sofa was still covered in all that Sonia had unearthed. The room was filled with thin grey light. It wasn't crackling she heard in the doorway but footsteps; afterwards she was sure that that was what she had heard first, and she half-wondered if there was someone else in the flat, if someone had got in. The thud of footsteps that got closer and closer, but the sound was coming out of the machine, out of the box cradled in the old woman's useless hands. Then the voice.

And when she had thus said, she turned herself back, and saw Jesus standing, and knew not that it was Jesus.

The voice got closer all the time, began as nothing and came close, stopped. Sonia stood there, the heat of the mug burning her hands, unable to go any nearer. There was no more sound than that; the whole city slept outside, beyond them.

Jesus saith unto her, Woman, why weepest thou? She, supposing him to be the gardener, saith unto him, Sir, if thou have borne him hence, tell me where thou hast laid him, and I will take him away.

Jesus saith unto her, Mary. She turned herself, and saith unto him, Rabboni, which is to say, Master.

Sonia dared to go closer, put the tea down at last on the bedside table. She went on noiseless feet, not daring to make a sound.

The Miracle

Sonia was neither a Protestant nor a Catholic; she was nothing. She believed in bricks through windows, she believed in the edges of knives, she believed in lies and betrayal.

But the voice went on; the story of a man who had been raised from the dead. A man who had been done away with, who had been murdered in cold blood. But Sonia did not stop; her eyes were on the radio, on that ancient Bakelite box with its creases of dust. She went closer and closer on soundless feet until she was as close to it as she could be and she knelt down on the floor, watching it all the time.

And then the singing began – a flow of voices as if in some ancient place. It brought something back to her – somewhere, a place she couldn't remember the name of. A red house and a wood and her father laughing. She could smell everything. He was carrying her up steep wooden steps, talking to her all the time and she had been crying. He wasn't angry any more and she felt safe, and she didn't want to go to sleep even after he'd kissed her goodnight. She wanted to lie there awake because she was happy and safe, and if she slept it would be tomorrow and a whole night would be lost and wasted.

*

The singing stopped and Sonia lifted her head. She'd put her face down into the bedclothes and closed her eyes, without even being aware of doing so. Now she lifted her head. She stared at the radio in the old woman's blue-veined hands and held her breath so she could hear everything. And she felt a peace she hadn't known since childhood, since that last night in the old house. And she looked at Marie's face, at the light there. It was as if the tiny face was shining.

And she heard steps, just like the steps she had heard when she stood in the doorway, except now they were going away; they were diminishing until they had disappeared completely. And there was nothing left, not even a hiss.

But all of that had come all the same: the steps, the voice, the singing. All of those places, all of those words. They had come from nowhere, yet perhaps they hadn't all the same. Suddenly she thought of something. Sonia reached out and took the radio, and Marie's hands did not resist; they fell away as if they had been pieces of candle wax. She took the radio and turned it over onto its back and found the little plastic clasp. She caught it with her fingernail and it came loose; the little black lid fell away onto the bedclothes. She stared in disbelief. In the little cave of the compartment there was nothing at all. There never had been anything.

She looked up at the old woman, the empty box that weighed nothing at all still held in her hands. And Marie's head had fallen forwards; her eyes were quite closed.

The Ice

For the last three miles of the drive, once onto the Hallion estate proper, Lewis felt as though he wasn't there. Perhaps it was the motion of the car on the bumpy track, and the warmth of the vehicle with its steamed-up windows; it felt as though his hands and feet melted away, and all he heard from somewhere far away was the engine's hum.

Harry had said nothing either: the odd thing when he met the boy at the station, about bags and boxes and what could go where. But somehow he sensed there was no point in more, about what Glenellen was like and how the first term had gone. Lewis sat, eyes fixed straight ahead, the crumpled coat still held under his right arm, there and yet not there at all.

Only when they passed the dark forest of rhododendron and swung round a wide bend did the boy seem to come alive. A sudden glint of silver through the birches, and he was wiping the misted window to see.

'Woodpeckers this morning,' Harry said, filling the silence. 'Two of them at the feeders behind the Lodge.'

But Lewis was looking away left, through the thinning trees to the grey expanse of water. He was there and yet not there, and when the tall white walls of the Lodge were finally visible, he unclipped the seatbelt and opened the door before Harry had properly stopped.

'Will you wait!' Harry exclaimed, but there was no point. The boy was running between tree roots and rusted clumps of bracken towards the water. The engine fluttered and died. A scattering of mallard scrabbled into the air, complaining. Harry sat there still, hearing the silence, watching the boy's silhouette against the grey-white water, till the back door of the Lodge banged and a tall man in a tweed jacket started over the gravel towards the car. Harry was out at once.

'You'll need to have a look at the fence above Croft Hill. Bloody deer through again. Have you time, Harry?'

A violin in its dark case was lifted carefully onto the track.

'Yes, sir, as soon as I've seen to the track. The flood's made a right mess.'

Suddenly the man looked down towards the water. The boy was still there, small and dark against the pale surface of the lake. Far out, over towards the opposite shore, was an islet, crowded with tall trees and dark shadows of undergrowth.

'And how's he?' the man asked, not looking round.

Harry paused, watching him. 'Seems fine. Eager to get down there!'

They both laughed and Harry started carting in bags. The man kept where he was and took out a cigarette; the blue smoke hung in the still air. When the first luggage went into the hall he heard a muffled voice from upstairs; Harry's name was all he made out. Then his mother appeared, looking round anxiously in every direction.

'Lewis!' she shouted. 'Where are you, Lewis?'

Her voice carried; echoed over the water to the far shore. The boy turned and began to run, almost as though there was no gap between turning and running. He flew up through the bracken in one sure line towards that voice.

The cigarette's thin blue coil drifted into the still air.

'Mind your coat, Lewis!'

He watched the boy as he ran, eyes dark, but the boy didn't look at him. As though he hadn't heard. He poured himself into the arms of the elderly woman in her wide skirts and checked jacket. She buried her hands in his hair.

*

He stayed on the couch in her sitting room till the clock in the hall fluttered seven times. He lay curled there, face turned away and buried in the cushion, as though fast asleep. She sat beside him a long time, her hand in the straight dark gold of his hair. He talked after he'd stopped crying; he talked in angry fragments about the Latin teacher, about Saturday nights after prep, about the way the matron treated him when he fell. But most of all he talked about swimming; the stone-cold place where they waited for Macgregor, and all that happened before he came. She felt there herself with those thin, white boys as the shouting echoed around the walls at those who still couldn't swim. Her fingers ran over the soft skin at the nape of his neck, and she brushed her hand fiercely over her eyes so he wasn't aware of her emotion.

'Lewis, it's time for dinner. You've not unpacked a thing and I haven't written my letter. Come on, you've barely seen your father!'

She moved but he didn't. She looked at him, curled there on the couch, and remembered him two years before, in the weeks after Kate died. This was where he'd come and this was how he'd lain – just the same, only a little smaller. And she heard again that crying she'd never forget; the long, slow wave of it, exhausted and broken, like some terrible song. He'd talked to her then too, and that was how he felt safest – turned away, head buried in the cushion and eyes closed, her hand at the back of his hair. She'd given him then a little white elephant her husband had once carved. He was dying when he made it for her; he said nothing but she knew it was to be a way of remembering him. Now it was for Lewis and no one else, to hold when he could endure no more – something to take back to Glenellen, to carry always. She remembered and sat down again beside him, her hand suddenly even gentler than before. He noticed and half-turned, not understanding, his face glassy and broken.

'Listen,' she said, taking hold of his hand instead. 'I have an idea. The island on the lake.'

Now he sat up, was watching her.

'Your grandfather had a house out there, you know. Not much more than a cabin, but when he was a child he called it the Christmas House. One winter he stayed there, when there was enough ice. It was something he never forgot. Why don't you go there this Christmas, with your brother and your cousin Winifred, if the ice is strong enough?'

'And stay out there?' Lewis asked, not blinking. 'Would we be able to stay out there?'

She nodded, almost regretting what she'd said, as her son called from downstairs that dinner was ready – had been for twenty minutes.

*

Roddy came home that Friday. Even though he was only fourteen he'd persuaded Harry to let him drive once they were off the main road. His father was checking pheasant pens and met them half a mile from the Lodge; he all but strung Roddy up, face pulped to purple fury. He didn't speak to Harry for two days, just left the sparsest notes for him in the porch.

Lewis felt strange when he saw his brother from the landing window, as though there were things to hide away. He felt confused and scared and didn't know why. But they laughed about Roddy getting caught, and that was all right. He wanted to tell him about the Christmas House, but he didn't.

'What was it like?' he asked instead.

Roddy looked up from his bags. 'The corps training? Awful, bad as it could have been. Fuzzy was in charge of my group. At least Macgregor wasn't there, though.'

Lewis felt his cheeks sting when he remembered Macgregor. Suddenly he smelled Glenellen again in the stale clothes Roddy spilled out over the floor. He wanted it gone, to have no place here, not to spoil what was precious.

That afternoon he ran up Croft Hill in the last light, all the way to the top, and stood there panting, palms on his knees. His father said you could see every corner of the estate from the summit. All Lewis wanted was to see the lake, and this was the best place. He dug out his grandfather's precious monocular from its chestnut case, crouched in the heather and forced his breathing to slow.

The magnified circle crossed the lake and found the islet. A beach on the near side, the one facing him. He followed what looked like a path further in, through birches and bushes to something round and wooden. He heard his heart. A window in the near side, small and thin, like in a castle. The very heart of the islet a tangle of trees and brambles. At the very far end a line of stones, and there on the last of them a heron, hunched grey. He was sure there was a rough ring made for a fireplace; suddenly pictured them years ago, not in the middle of winter at all but at midsummer. The night blue and the orange glow of a fire lighting their faces; laughter echoing over the water and someone daring them to swim. They'd pulled off all their clothes and crashed into the water, splashing and laughing as the rest of them watched, applauding.

*

That night Lewis was back at Glenellen. There among a wandered tangle of dreams, dense as the island's heart. Back in the first week; the first day of swimming. He heard the drip as they waited, twenty-four white figures; feet together, toes touching the pool edge. Like the drip of time itself.

A prefect was there in uniform. Mr Macgregor would be over shortly; this was a chance to talk about a gala happening in October. An inter-house gala; they all knew the importance of representing their houses? Twenty-four heads nodded and the drip ticked, ticked. The boy's black shoes echoed dully on the cold stone as he paced up and down at the deep end.

How many would still be twelve on the thirteenth of October?
A flutter of hands. How many were thirteen now?

Lewis was confused, kept his hand up after the others had
fallen, and the prefect noticed. The shoes stopped. His question echoed.

'Please, sir, it's my birthday today. What should I do?'

A smile spread over the prefect's face, like flame across paper.

'What should you do? Well, to begin with, you shouldn't call
me sir.' A slow snigger from twenty-three figures, suddenly
watching and enjoying. 'Secondly, you should come up here.'

Lewis was right down at the shallow end. He obeyed, bare feet
treading the shimmer of thin pools on the stone. He didn't
understand. He was freezing.

The prefect was grinning. He had bad breath. 'What's your
name?'

'Lewis. I mean Cameron.'

'Right, Cameron, happy birthday!'

The prefect lifted him as if he was nothing more than balsa
wood, carried him up to the top diving board, and tipped him
out into the deep end. Lewis came to the surface, swallowing

and choking, arms swirling to reach the side, the laughter and applause sore in his ears. He couldn't swim.

*

That Sunday there was a party at the Lodge. The last rain was gone and the skies luminous blue. Not a whisper of sound by the lake; a twig cracked underfoot and the echo seemed to carry like a gunshot. It would freeze that night: the first frost. Lewis turned and looked over at the islet; nothing more than a dark shadow hunched on the water's surface, the taller trees searching like dark hands into the sky. *This was going to be the first night of frost.* His heart sang.

The boys ate at a table set by their grandmother.

'Why can't we come to the party?' Roddy asked through a mouthful of venison.

'Because you can't,' his father said, looking out of the side window onto the track, a cigarette in his right hand. He didn't look round.

The cars came in soft curves up the track, headlights turning the hillsides vivid gold. Voices and laughter warm in the yard; plumes of white breath clouding the night, a night that left diamonds on sills and roofs. Lewis watched from the window of their bedroom and missed his mother so badly it felt sore as a rusty knife. He found the elephant in his pocket; dug it into his palm. He yearned for her. Whenever he remembered she filled him like a gust of longing and he felt blown out of himself. Nothing in the world mattered then but that longing.

The cars shone below under a cold ball of moon like a single eye. Everyone had arrived; the downstairs rooms flowed with talk and laughter, the clink of cutlery and glasses.

Roddy came over to the window and opened it.

'Look,' he hissed, brought out a miniature of whisky and a cigarette. 'Got them from Dad.' In answer to the loud question in Lewis' white face.

He didn't enjoy either, though he pretended to. He was too terrified of his grandmother appearing at the door, of the consequences. He just felt sick and dizzy.

He ate mints and brushed his teeth twice, scrubbed his face as though scraping moss from stone, and gargled. He lay awake long after Roddy's breath grew soft and easy; the car doors thudded and the goodnights were loud outside. He padded onto the landing and looked for his grandmother; sat there, crouching and shivering. At last she appeared, wheezing, one hand slow on the banister, turning to go up her own stair.

'How thick does the ice have to be, Granny?' he whispered.

She looked round, paused, not understanding at once. Then her eyes lit and she smiled. 'Three and a half inches.'

*

John Cameron was up before dawn. He'd not slept well, had what his own father called a whisky head. He went out into the blue stillness, coat buttoned against the cold. It must have been five below during the night. He heard something in the trees at the back of the Lodge: the ragged voices of greylag. He heard them but couldn't see them and remembered the last goose he'd shot the year before, over on the lake's far shore. He'd found it, flapping and broken, its long neck stretched for breath. It was trying so hard, flailing, and in that second he remembered Kate, two days before she died in the white lie of that city hospital. He'd looked down at the goose and something broke in him too.

He went down to the lake. The bracken bristled with frost; sharp panes of ice crackled underfoot. It was beginning to grow grey; he saw the lake edge as he came close. A white skin of ice. He extended one foot and heard the sound as it crackled; it was thicker than he'd imagined, though further out the water remained black and clear. They'd said it would be a hard winter: maybe Lewis would get his wish. He smiled ironically. His mother shouldn't have filled the boy's head with hope all the same; what chance was there of that kind of ice? They'd made the lake a hundred years and more ago for curling; back then it could be frozen solid for weeks.

The cabin on the island, built by his great-grandfather for those curling matches. For a hot toddy and a glowing brazier on days when hands turned to raw, red, useless stumps. His father christened it the Christmas House; several winters running he'd gone out there as a boy, taking all he needed over the ice.

How long since winters like that? John Cameron bent for a shard of ice. This might be all they'd get. He skimmed it away and stood tall, suddenly cold himself. The hills grew from the darkness. Up beside the Lodge he heard the soft riches of a blackbird's song, so beautiful he had to stop. And he remembered another blackbird, however long ago, singing in the back courts of the city. He'd stood and listened, made up his mind that when his studies were done he'd return to Hallion after all, and with his Kate.

*

'Why is Winifred coming for Christmas?' Roddy asked at breakfast. 'Don't they celebrate Christmas in Manchester?'

His father folded his paper and just looked at him.

Their grandmother put down the teapot. 'Winifred is coming because her parents are going to the Lake District, and they decided for a treat she should come north to us, which is why it's up to you to make sure her time is special.'

Lewis hadn't seen his cousin since his mother died. She'd been there at the church, had shaken his hand on the way out. He remembered her eyes, her very brown eyes – that was all. She'd said nothing; just looked right at him, as though saying something nonetheless.

'That's not the reason Winifred's coming,' Roddy said upstairs, thumping onto his bed and yawning. 'I heard Gran talking to her parents yonks ago; they're probably getting a divorce. I reckon they're off to get peace and quiet, sort it all out.'

Lewis thought about that, and about Winifred's brown eyes, when he went up to the attic. He'd tidied his room, but was to wait in the house until Winifred arrived.

The skylight window was covered with crystals of frost. He stared up at a patterning of thousands of gems. He couldn't see the sky, it was so frosted.

He started rummaging through an old box of stuff, gathered from castles and lodges and boats. He bounced a rubber ball against the wall till it leapt away and started down the stairs. Some of his father's rugby shirts from Glenellen; his name in Gothic script along the inside of the collar. It felt strange to touch them.

He pulled out a black radio: held it, thinking. Inside were voices from every corner of the globe. Sometimes far away, as though trying to speak through a storm of crackling, then suddenly clear as if there in the same room. This would be dead for certain.

He clicked the dial nonetheless and bent to listen. Not even a crackling; just a distant hiss. It was somehow like mist, but that wasn't a sound. He turned the dial very slowly; sometimes the mist lessened, and perhaps there was the ghost of a voice. He kept on, bent right over, his ear hard against the radio, hoping.

And suddenly a voice, every word clear:

'. . . *for England and Wales much the same story. About five or six in sheltered parts, but several degrees warmer elsewhere, especially along the south coast. In Scotland the weather's set to get much colder as high pressure moves in from Scandinavia; tonight we could be looking at a dip to minus ten . . .*'

Lewis clicked off the radio and the voice was gone. He crouched there, his heart singing.

*

'Train an hour and a half late. Heavy snow in the Lakes.'

Harry staggered in with a case, several odd-shaped parcels and a thinly disguised bottle which John Cameron helped to safety.

'Winifred, you must be exhausted! Come in, dear, and welcome. You remember Roddy, and Lewis would have been an inch smaller when you last saw him.'

The brown eyes just as he remembered. Like a parcel herself, wrapped in Manchester against the legendary Scottish cold. Granny Cameron wound away layer after layer as Winifred smiled and watched; the boys standing there, feet shuffling.

'Come on, then! Show your cousin some courtesy! Off up and get warm, Winifred, and make sure they look after you. Yes, take Winifred to her room first, Roddy, and then come down when you're ready. We'll restore you with tea and cake!'

As night began falling, Lewis asked if she'd like to see the lake. The brown eyes nodded. His heart thudded, but he felt all right, and he had to show her. Outside, stars sparked above them. They stood in the fierce blue cold.

'You can't really see stars in Manchester,' she said. 'Not like that.'

Her head was turned right up to look; in the light of the porch lamp he saw the gold hair that curled about her eyes.

'Come on,' he said. 'You have to see the lake!'

Almost as if he'd made it himself. He forgot to go as his father would have, slowly and carefully; he chased through bracken and long grass, forgetting everything. But she ran too and they reached the shore together.

'Out there's an island,' he said, the cold catching his breath. 'Further over to the right. There's a place on it called the

Christmas House. If we get enough ice we can spend Christmas there; we can stay there.'

He looked to see what she thought. Her eyes were bright – he didn't need to ask.

'So you'll come, Winifred, if it freezes?'

She looked at him, nodding as though he was stupid.

'And I hate Winifred,' she said. 'Call me Winnie like everyone else.'

*

Lewis drifted in a no-man's-land between sleeping and waking. He knew he wasn't in the boarding house; somewhere deep inside he felt back home. He'd worked out the night before that twelve more days remained; if he counted the drive to the station and the train journey then twelve and a half. He'd fallen asleep with twelve and a half days safe in his head; they rocked him to sleep. And he dreamed a real winter came, the sort there'd once been, when forty or fifty degrees of frost locked everything in a white fist of ice.

He walked through Glenellen rejoicing because there could be no more classes, because everyone had gone. He found himself beside the swimming pool and the water was solid white ice. He'd never have to learn to swim again. Then he turned and Winnie was there. Her brown eyes held him and she began running – out from the frozen pool onto the playing fields. Into the trees beside them till he saw the shape of the Lodge peeping between the birches, the grey-white shimmer of lake behind. She'd brought him home . . .

He felt someone shaking him and calling his name, but he didn't want to be dragged from his dream. They kept tugging and tugging him.

'Lewis! Lewis, it's me!' It was his granny, and he knew it must be very early. The room still half-dark; in the other bed the unmistakable hump of Roddy's back. She set a cup of hot orange on his bedside table; he recognized the scent. She'd made it each morning when his mum was so ill in hospital. And she'd put her hand through his hair.

He struggled to sit up, his face all crumpled with sleep. He heard her smile.

'The ice is thick enough. You can go out to the island tonight.'

*

At five Harry went over the ice: they all went down to watch. John Cameron was closest to the shore, the firefly of his cigarette flickering the blue dark. Already eight below. He finished giving instructions about the path that led to the House, and suddenly the quiet fell and Harry set off. His boots thudded the ice; the light of his head torch zigzagging as his shadow grew into the night. Lewis thought of the story of Jesus walking on water, and suddenly realized that what he'd dreamed had happened after all. His father had been wrong; the ice was thick enough and they were going to the Christmas House. Winnie was beside him; he caught the scent of her, was sure of it. He closed his eyes, felt he couldn't breathe for joy. *It was going to happen.*

'I'm there!' Harry's call reached them; echoed over the ice and hung in the stillness. And they came alive again, the listeners; they shuffled their freezing feet, started talking – John Cameron to his mother with the lantern by the shore, Roddy to Winifred so she laughed. Harry's head torch flashed in the trees, a single beam of brightness. Then, as they turned back to the Lodge, that light vanished too. Lewis was the last to turn. Harry had found the path.

*

Granny Cameron came to see them off. Lewis went first with such a bundle he almost couldn't see where he was going. He tried to look all the same; not just ahead but around him – up into the hill opposite, silver-plated with moonlight, the pines eerie white with their jewellery of frost. He caught the wary eyes of hinds in a clearing low down, ears like bears' – half-moons of listening. They watched and then, as though on cue, turned and scattered.

'Not so fast! Wait for me!' Winnie protested.

He stood, waiting and happy. The Lodge lights cast vague gold trails over the ice. Roddy had barely set out, was trying to carry all that remained despite his grandmother's chiding.

'Did you tell your parents?' Lewis suddenly asked when she'd caught up with him.

'Tell them what?' She kept her eyes on the ice.

'About coming here. That we'd come here.'

She shook her head. 'They were busy with everything. I don't remember. Look at Roddy! He can hardly walk!'

Her laughter rang out and echoed, and for a moment Lewis wanted to tell her she was breaking the quiet. She'd turned back a few steps, as though wanting to help Roddy. Granny Drummond was making her way slowly up towards the Lodge; she'd told Lewis to *remember every second*.

So Winnie and he reached the island first: the little beach he'd seen from the top of Croft Hill. They fought between trees, trying to follow something that might once have been a path. It was difficult, even in the steel whiteness of the moonlight. Lewis broke his way onwards, stabbed by branches.

A spray of shadows brushed back against Winnie's face. 'Is it much further?'

He didn't answer because suddenly they were there, in a little glade encircled by pine trees and dense undergrowth. They were there and the cabin stood right in front of them. A plume of maroon smoke curled from the roof; the fire inside popped and whined. *Good old Harry.*

But the door had broken and the only thing was to crawl under what remained. Lewis looked inside, from the vantage point of his knees. The one thin window; the red roar of fire. They left their loads and crawled. Winnie went to the window to look out.

'It could be Siberia!' she breathed. 'Look, Lewis!'

He hunched there too, head bent close to hers. *Like in an advent calendar*, he thought. The moon high over the trees; the lake with its silver patternings, a white floor of whorls and paths.

'Can't you imagine wolves?' Winnie said. 'Wolves coming across, hunting? As if it could be any time; I mean ages ago. Like walking into a story, a story you once read!'

Then Roddy arrived, and they struggled to bring rugs in, light lamps and make up beds. All their toes would point in to the middle. Roddy built a great stack of wood and it smelled like mushrooms. They barricaded the broken door, then lay in the darkness listening to the fire. Roddy said he'd get up at three to make sure it was still alight; he always woke anyway, and he'd rebuild it so it was going in the morning.

Lewis didn't want to sleep, but lie somewhere between waking and sleeping, the thump and hiss of the fire in his ears. *They had got to the island; it had happened.*

He slept just the same, though his dreaming felt real enough. He woke and the fire was dead. The Christmas House was filled with silver light, shone on the face of Winnie next to him, and on Roddy who was furthest away. She was facing him, on her side, and might have been sculpted from silver. He couldn't even hear the sound of her breathing. He got up, slipped out, glided over the ice towards the Lodge lying in darkness, asleep. He crept inside, found his fiddle case, took the violin and went back out into the very middle of the lake and began playing. And creatures came alive and gathered at the edge of the ice to listen; deer and pine martens with their gorgeous orange tummies, and long-snouted badgers. Last of all, Winnie came out of the Christmas House, smiling, and he turned towards her, for it was for her he really had played.

*

The three of them were up at nine. Roddy hadn't woken after all in the night and the fire was a mess of charred ends of wood. They could see their breath. Lewis pulled on his clothes, juddering, fingers like whittled twigs. They didn't speak: their mouths locked and sore. Lewis crawled under the broken door, everything covered in white like cobwebs. The Lodge gone; a carpet of mist over the lake hiding the shore from them. He whirled his arms and bashed his red hands against his sides.

Then he heard Winnie; saw her standing laughing at him help-lessly. He smiled, shy, and remembered his dream.

It took thirty-six matches and a great deal of blowing to coax the fire back to life. For the next hour they did little but huddle in the room, watching the flames.

'What's that box?' Winnie asked at last. She'd noticed some-thing under one of the ledges, something they hadn't brought with them over the ice. They looked, reluctant to move. Lewis finally struggled up, feet still freezing, and slid it out – covered with dust and ash, like something that had survived a volcano, belonged to another world. He swept his hand over the top to clear it.

'The Christmas Box,' he read. He brought it over, not opening it till he was there. Winnie took out a velvet bag that rattled; she struggled with the drawstring, poured a collection of sheep and shepherds and kings and angels into her hands. They were white and roughly carved, all the size of her thumb.

'I bet Granddad did those,' Roddy said, leaning over, and glanced at Lewis. 'Gran's still got his favourite knife, the one with the mother-of-pearl handle.'

And Lewis thought of the elephant in his pocket, made of the same white wood. He remembered the knife from his gran's bedroom they'd been allowed to pick up and look at, but never take away.

Winnie set the nativity figures on the stonework beside the fire. Firelight played on the faces. There were candles in the box, and one or two ancient Christmas cards; half a dozen pine cones dry and fragile with age, light as air. They brought out everything with a kind of puzzled reverence, as the mist swept at last from the lake and the morning turned a fierce white-blue, one single pane of light.

*

It was Christmas Eve and Granny Cameron brought down a box of skates from the attic. They'd been hers, and would do for Winnie, and after much rummaging there was a pair for Lewis too. Roddy assured them he'd only break a leg; that would mean no cricket for the whole next season. Instead he found Tosca and Rascal, took them running up Croft Hill.

'Watch that bit at the bottom of the island,' John Cameron called over the ice. 'Not sure I'd trust it. Keep over here, between the Lodge and the top.'

Lewis heard, but he was calling and whooping. He fell and it hurt but he laughed, at the blue sky and Winnie's face smiling down at him. And Granny Cameron stood at the shore, arms folded tightly against the frozen air, remembering how he'd been just two years before – broken and bereft, like a bird that wouldn't fly again. She'd never wanted him to go to Glenellen; fought hard with her son against that. She well knew what awaited him there; how ill prepared he was. But she was never going to have the last word; knew she would lose in the end. Yet he was here now, and that was all that mattered.

Later they trailed inside for mulled wine. Roddy came back with Tosca and Rascal and the story of a fox; then they sat and grazed, as Granny Cameron put it – sprouts and ham, tea. The light gathered itself to crystal white, and Lewis watched through the window as six wood pigeons ruffled soundlessly from the trees on the far lake shore, blinked into that whiteness and were gone. His granny was suddenly beside him.

'May we come over and join you this evening?' she asked. It was his permission she'd sought, and he noticed. His face shone.

'If you bring a present.'

She thought for a moment. 'Why don't we open all our presents there, all our family ones?'

So they did. Roddy and Lewis took an arm each because she was afraid of falling; John Cameron came behind with a sledge laden with parcels, and the bottle of his favourite malt from Winnie's parents.

The fire was coaxed into life and the candles lit so a lemony light filled the Christmas House. They blocked the gap in the door as best they could so it felt like an igloo. That was what Lewis suddenly thought.

'We should have Harry with us,' Granny Cameron said, looking over at her son. 'We could have given him his present here. Still, I expect he's perfectly content with his family.'

'And with a large bottle of brandy, if I know Harry Cartwright,' John added. 'What about presents, then? If my arms don't have movement soon they're liable to get frostbite. Shall I be Father Christmas?'

Winnie had hers first, since she was the guest; a present she knew at once was a book. A copy of *Swiss Family Robinson*, something she had – but this was much nicer-looking, and she didn't let on. The other parcel soft and small; she squashed it to guess.

'They're going to come in pretty handy,' her uncle winked, and that was true. They were sheepskin gloves, and Winnie put them on then and there.

Roddy got a new satchel for fishing; examined every pocket and compartment. Granny Cameron had only brought her presents from the boys; Roddy had made her a bird table in woodwork, Lewis a toast rack.

'Your grandfather would be proud of you,' she told them.

'Just don't eat your breakfast from the wrong one,' her son told her, throwing another log on the fire. 'There's a parcel for you, Lewis, one from me.'

It weighed nothing, was wrapped in grey paper. He opened it carefully, remembering always he hadn't to tear the paper.

'For heaven's sake, put us out of our misery!' his father said, and Lewis felt his face reddening, thinking of Winnie.

He opened the little box and it was a pair of swimming trunks; blue, with a white stripe down one side.

'For when you can swim! Later this year!'

'You mean next year, Dad,' Roddy pointed out.

'All right, whatever, next year.'

Lewis said thank you, but he felt far away, as if someone else spoke the words inside and the real him shrank and shrank. The talk around him became one single voice and all the words melted together.

Later, when the three islanders crawled out and said goodnight to their visitors, and they'd barricaded the door again and built up the fire into a golden dome of flame, he took the swimming trunks and buried them in his bag so they were gone, so they weren't there any more.

'Where are you, Lewis?' Winnie asked, tapping his head playfully, as the three of them sipped sweet cocoa in the burning glare of the fire.

'I'm here,' he murmured, but he knew it wasn't true all the same. He tried with all his might to clamber back into himself and return, to the only place he wanted to be. But he kept falling away, hearing the drip, drip in his head that dragged him back. He kept remembering though all he wanted to do was forget, even when they went to bed at last, and he lay awake long after he yearned to sleep.

*

It was partridge they had that Christmas afternoon, when the Lodge clock had fluttered four times, and they sat round the table at last with its red napkins and white candles.

Granny Cameron looked older. Lewis suddenly realized that; she sat opposite him in her white dress with the topaz brooch her husband had brought back from Ceylon after his war was over. It glittered like the blue of her eyes, but she was older just the same. It was as though it had happened while he was away, and he felt an overwhelming desire to hold her and not let her go.

He watched Winnie as she sat talking to his father; he was leaning close to her and she was nodding, her brown eyes bright. He knew he should look away but he couldn't; then she seemed to know and glanced at him and their eyes met. Just a flash and he looked away, shy, and she and his father were laughing. He wanted there to be time; to go up into the wood to look for red squirrels, to take her up Croft Hill. If there was enough moonlight they could go sledging.

'Gran, can I get something from the island?'

He'd remembered the Christmas box. He wanted to show her the figures his grandfather had carved, know if she had seen them before.

His feet hissed through the white bracken. Out onto the ice and now the sky was a mingling of white and blue and yellow. He wished he could paint and capture it. He stopped, there in the middle of the pathway of ice, gulping air into his lungs. He wanted to walk into that light and never stop.

He brought back everything in the end; somehow he wanted things just as when Winnie found the box and opened it. For his grandmother to see exactly what it had been like. But when he emerged on hands and knees, the box held awkwardly in front of him, the air was dark blue and the light gone. He'd been no time at all yet it had passed.

The box was heavier than he'd imagined, banged against his thighs as he carried it so he had to walk slowly. He felt every step as he trudged the hillside to the Lodge.

'Lewis?'

He'd not seen his father in the shadows: jumped, didn't answer. His father had come out for a smoke.

'I want you into the house tonight. It's to be milder by the morning. Another half-hour then go over and get all your stuff.'

The words echoed inside him. He felt his face burn with anguish and frustration and rage. He wanted to rail at his father as he turned away. *It wasn't fair, it was wrong, he couldn't.* The words melted into crying; a tangle of angry sobs, words that no longer made any sense. He chucked the box on the ground and crouched, folded into himself, weeping as he'd done when he was four. *He couldn't take this away; it wasn't his and he didn't have the right. He didn't care.* Lewis hugged his arms about his chest and looked down, searching, to the lake. But the island was gone, swallowed by dark.

*

Now the Lodge was quiet; all the lights were out. Roddy's soft snore was like a whine; along the corridor their father had finally gone to bed. Lewis had heard Winnie closing her door and hadn't been able to put her out of his mind. He remembered her scent and sat there on the floor in the darkness, wondering. Then he thought of the Christmas House and glanced away, wanting to escape the prison of his own head. He would drive himself mad. He had left last; by then Roddy was out onto the ice with rugs and boxes, calling impatiently for him to hurry. He hadn't had time to say goodbye.

On the floor beside him were the swimming trunks. The white stripe showed in the darkness. He felt back at Glenellen on a morning in mid-October. He could hear Macgregor . . .

'All right, there's room for an awful lot of improvement; I'm pretty disappointed with the lot of you. Now I've to be at a meeting in exactly eight and a half minutes, so out in two and shower. Ditchfield, you are my eyes and ears. One scrap of trouble and I want to know. Understood?'

'Yes, sir.'

The plimsolls squeaked along the changing-room corridor as Macgregor disappeared. The sound of the ticking drip of water. Then the outer door banged and the place erupted: echoes of shrieking and laughter, water being cuffed and bodies dive-bombing the deep end. Ditchfield shouted something at George Fife; shouting was the only way of making yourself heard. *If only he'd come back*, Lewis thought. *If only he'd hear.*

But he didn't. In two minutes they began dragging themselves out, knowing the period bell was looming. As Lewis was clambering out at the shallow end, he felt hands at his shoulders pulling him back. For a confused second he saw a sea of faces above as he was ducked in the water; the piercing shrieks hurt his ears as he went under and struggled up, fighting his way through them and gasping for breath.

'Where d'you get the trunks, Cameron? Your mother?'

The showers were already on when he got out. Someone singing; the sound of someone else farting. He returned to his cubicle as slowly as he could, dragged down his sodden trunks and picked up his towel. His heart hurt in his chest. He walked into the sweat and the steam.

'Here he is, lads! Make way for the great swimmer!'

He saw Ditchfield in front, a whole head taller than himself. He looked at him with nothing less than hatred: his eyes black.

'What's that between your legs, Cameron? Is it real or just stuck on? Shall we find out, lads?'

Ditchfield whipped his towel from a hook at the side of the showers. The jackals started clapping, cheering and clapping. On the other side and out of the corner of his eye, Lewis saw another towel. He glanced at the clock, willing the minute hand to move. Still another four and a half minutes to the bell. They'd trapped him. He couldn't get back to his own towel.

Ditchfield dipped the end of his in water and twisted it, taking all the time he wanted. He practised a flick; let the towel crack in the air in front of him. The slow clapping increased; a murmur of expectation and delight. Ditchfield moved closer.

A towel came at Lewis from another corner and he reached out pathetically with one hand. He felt the cold gust of air. An echo of mirth went up at his attempt to save himself. He glanced at

Ditchfield, eyes pleading, felt his own back against metal. He couldn't go any further.

Ditchfield aimed at his groin and Lewis clutched at himself. The wet tongue of towel stung against his hands and was gone. How many seconds to the bell? How many seconds to go? The other towel came to distract him again and he swung round, enraged and humiliated. And Ditchfield took aim. The lightning fork flickered in the air and there was an audible crack as it hit. Lewis screamed and crumpled onto the tiles. A cheer rang out; echoed through the whole building.

Ditchfield turned to get dressed, waving his towel in victory. And as they melted away, the bell rang at last.

*

He held the trunks in his hands. If there were thirty weeks of term each year, and he had two periods of swimming a week, that meant three hundred before leaving Glenellen. There was no way out.

He heard something, a muffled sound from Winnie's room, and held his breath. It was ten past twelve; Christmas Day was over. He listened and realized that Winnie was crying. Like a soft, slow wave; the way he'd cried when his mother died. He'd thought then of a story, of a child whose mother dies and who goes down to the underworld to ask if ever she might be restored. *Oh yes*, was the answer, *if you weep a whole river of tears, and that river flows here into the darkness, she'll be restored.* So he returned and wept until the river was enough. But it wasn't true.

Lewis got up, the swimming trunks still in his hand. He held the door handle, turned it softly to keep the house's quiet. He knew how to do it right; the door sighed and he went into the corridor on soft feet. He listened outside Winnie's door; saw no edge of light showing from inside. He didn't knock, just turned the handle and slid the door open.

She sat up in bed, trying to smudge away her tears.

'I heard you,' he breathed, and sat down at the bottom of the bed. He began to see her face; she grew out of the dark.

'Sorry,' she whispered, but he shook his head. That wasn't what he had meant; that wasn't why he had come.

She looked down for a second, into the net of her hands, then met his eyes again.

'I was crying because of my mum and dad. I don't want to go home because I know what's there. This was like a dream, and now it's over. They're divorcing, and I've to go and live with Mum in America. She's going back there.'

Lewis nodded and felt something break inside. There was something he had dared hope, or dared begin to hope – like a bridge, or like ice even. He'd believed he could walk over, that it would hold, and now that too was breaking. He was sinking and he couldn't even cry out.

'When I go home, I've to start packing. I've to get ready for a whole new world.'

Suddenly he thought of something, one small thing. He searched in his pocket and brought out the little elephant his grandfather had carved. He held it in his fingers, then dropped it into her empty hands.

'That's for you,' he said. 'For when you feel you can't go on. Hold it and believe. Don't forget.'

He half-stood and then bent forwards through the soft dark and laid his cheek against hers, just and no more. He caught her scent and closed his eyes.

'Goodbye,' he whispered.

'Goodbye,' she breathed, not understanding, her word more like a question. Then he was gone; before she could speak again he had turned away, as though swimming through the room's shadow and flowing from her world into somewhere else, and she had to touch her cheek to believe he had been there at all.

He went downstairs, his hand a hiss on the banister. In the porch he found his shoes and slipped them on. A rain thin as soft hair over the woods and the Hallion hills. He turned and went round the side of the track, down the slope towards the lake through the frost-sculpted grass and bracken. They jagged his ankles like tiny swords. Just once he looked back, up at Granny Cameron's window, but it was dark and empty, like a blind eye.

He didn't stop; he went on down to the bottom and out over the ice, the way Harry had gone that first day. He looked for the Christmas House but it was lost in dark and rain, as though it had never been. He went on, his feet making not a sound, till he'd reached the rocks at the end of the island. The ice creaked. He smiled and stopped, took off his clothes till he stood sculpted white and pure in the moonlight. Then he put on the new trunks.